1/89

Dear Ron + Bob,

I hope you enjoy this little book as much as I did!

Craig

THE BEAT

Born in England, Simon Payne grew up in outback Australia, wasting most of his youth in Alice Springs. After graduating from Flinder's University, he finally settled in Melbourne where he began writing. *The Beat* is his first published novel.

SIMON PAYNE

THE BEAT

First published April 1985 by GMP Publishers Ltd
P O Box 247, London N15 6RW, England.

Distributed in North America by Alyson Publications Inc.,
40 Plympton St, Boston, MA 02118, USA.

British Library Cataloguing in Publication Data

Payne, Simon
The beat.
I. Title
823[F] PR9619.3.P3/

ISBN 0-907040-70-5

Typeset by MC Typeset, Chatham, Kent, England.
Printed and bound by Billing and Sons Ltd,
Worcester, England.

I would like to thank the Australian Gay Archives for letting me use their resources in writing Chapter One, and also Richard Dipple, my editor at GMP, for his advice and encouragement.

Friday Night

It wasn't the first time Kevin had been poofter–bashing. They went quite often on a Friday night after drinking at the pub. If they didn't write themselves off and obliterate the week-end to come, they would go on a hunt of all the dunnies for a bit of sport. Poofters were pretty easy game and never squealed to the police after. They'd never done any real harm, it was just sport. One queer had got a pretty busted jaw the other week. It wobbled funny when he tried to speak and blood oozed from it. More like a fanny than a mouth by the time they had finished. A fanny needing rags.

Heads and balls usually got most of the punishment. Taught the queer bastards a lesson. That was what they used most, heads and balls, so that was what you went for. Stopped them practising their perverted ways for quite a while. Doing them a favour, and society too, keeping them out of the dunnies. You can't molest small boys if you have a pain in your gut because your stomach's been kicked in. They learn. They learn slow but they learn. Trouble is that there's always lots more to take their place.

There was this one guy they'd chased in the car one night. Spotlighting. Shit, you should have seen him run. He was so fast, dodging in and out of the headlights as they'd got him halfway across the park. They would have got him too, if it hadn't been for a tree that caused them to swerve and lose him. He went to ground so fast they lost him just like that. Cunning bastards, some of these poofters. Disappeared "poof" into the air, that's what Kevin would say.

They should have chased him on foot but some of these

queers are fast. All jogging around with their cocks trailing out of their shorts, as they run from dunnie to dunnie. It's getting harder to pick some of them these days. You can tell when they stand around limp-like, or when they speak, but it's hard to pick them on the run. Best way is to speak to them first, get their confidence; then when they speak back – whammo!

Kevin and his mate had got one the other day. He was walking along the footpath – must have been as blind as a bat. Broad daylight, there he was coming towards them, not looking at anyone. You could tell he was one of them by the way he walked, sort of like he had his knees tied together. Anyway, when he was about ten feet away, Kevin and his mate could see he was trying to stick to the fence, thinking he would get past them on that side. Kevin's mate moved over right up to the fence, so the poof had to pass between them. Just as he was going through, not looking at anyone, they closed in and knocked into him real hard. He reeled. For a second it looked as if he would lose his balance, but on he stumbled along the street. Didn't even look back at them.

"Ah," Kevin yelled.

He took no notice. So Kevin yells again. The silly bastard turns and looks.

"Yes?" he says, polite as he could.

"Don't you look where you're going?" Kevin yelled.

The guy shrugged and turned. Kevin steps towards him.

"You bumped my mate," he says. "What you got to say?"

"Sorry," says the poof, as if it doesn't matter, but you can see it does.

"You better be careful, uh?" says Kevin.

"OK," says the poof.

Again he turns and starts to walk away.

"You going to let him get away with that?" says Kevin's mate.

"Watch out, you fucking cunt," yells Kevin.

And the poof starts to walk real fast.

"I'll be after you," shouts Kevin. Then he starts making these funny poofter whooping noises.

The poof just hightailed and ran. That was the last they saw of that cunt.

It was usually good for a laugh. Kevin used to call it getting his exercise. He knew more about doing the dunnies than most of the queers did. It was no good starting too early, and you had to look out for police cars. Sometimes they would come interfering and you wouldn't see any queers again for weeks. They would all move on to somewhere new and you'd have to cruise around until you spotted them.

Kevin used to say he could smell them from the Aramis in the air. Maybe he could. For sure he could spot them even in the dark. He would see them under the trees strolling around. Out like possums at night. Avoided all the lights and just hung around in the shadows. Sometimes you could spot them having it off up against one of the trees, or some guy down sucking another's tool while the second guy went lookout. Funny they looked, peering round with some guy slobbering over their meat. They would get carried away and that was when they wouldn't notice you coming.

Up through the trees and whammo. Or you would see them tearing off with their tools still out, swinging before them like 'roos running backwards.

They'd tried mugging poofters for the bread at one stage, but it was useless. They all left their wallets in their cars. You could thump into them – but steal their bread, no way. Seemed strange the way they were so careful about that and careless about themselves – not smart at all really. No such thing as a smart poofter, it stood to reason. If you were smart you wouldn't be a poofter.

It was Friday night and they were pissed. Kevin had been at the pub since six. They had stopped drinking to have a counter meal. One of the guys had thrown it almost straight up, shit food that it was. He'd only just made it to the dunnie. Then he had sat there and moaned a bit. Kevin had reckoned he'd found a mate in there, he was gone so long. He was looking pretty bad now, just sitting quiet in the corner.

The rest of them weren't that bad. Until the last hour there had been some chicks there and the guys had kept sober enough to try and con onto them. But then they had gone off and now only the drinkers were left.

Kevin wanted to kick on a bit and have some fun. One of the guys was making noises about going home to his wife. Said he wanted to screw her senseless. He probably just wanted to rest, collapse at home. He had to keep his wits about him because he was getting the train. You couldn't let yourself doze off on those things, not with the way they were these days. In the past he had fallen asleep and been woken up in time for his stop, but these days drunks got mugged courtesy of Vic-Rail as they slept their way home. He had to go soon.

There was no one much to kick on. Kevin's best mate was still standing up but the one that had spewed was a write-off and so was this married guy. Just the two of them wanted to go on.

"Me car's up near the market," Kevin said. "Reckon you can make it?"

They half carried their corpse friend out into the street where the cold air hit him. For a moment he looked like he'd collapse.

The married one left them. He was a bit quiet too. A bit scared he would have to get off at each stop. The vibration of the train sometimes made you chuck after a few drinks. He'd known it before. You could feel alright till the thing started to move – whoops, and away you would go, redecorate the carriage in a stream of spew.

They got the corpse as far as the traffic lights. He hung onto the pole and wouldn't cross. Then he sort of folded up into a heap at the base, still clinging on. He reckoned the ground was nice and cool and he needed to cool off. They got him to his feet and across the lights. He could walk when he concentrated.

"I'll be no good for footie on Sunday," he moaned. The

thought sobered him a little and he staggered forward.

"Did aerobics on the oval on Thursday," he mused. "Did this guy's back in," and he stumbled. "Shit, help us one of you bastards."

"Aerobics is for poofs." Kevin spat.

It hit the ground in front of him and sat in a wet globule on the cold surface.

"Not the way we do it," the drunk persisted. "No poofs at footie."

"Bunch of fairies."

It was Kevin's last word on the subject and he flicked his mate in the crotch to make his point.

"Watch it," the drunk retorted, bending over in supposed pain. By now he could feel practically nothing. "You nearly ruined me." He lurched on up the street in the wake of his mates. "Where the fuck's this car?"

The third one had been fairly quiet until now. "Fucked if I know", came the reply, and they looked around bewildered.

"Oh yeah, I know," said Kevin and they were off again lurching up the street.

Their mate's mother wasn't too pleased when they dropped him off. They had to stay and hold him under the shower, she wasn't touching him in that state. He wouldn't let them take his jocks off, said they were a bunch of poofters, but had just crouched under the jets of water in his own vomit. When they got him out most of it had washed down the plughole. His old lady could clean up the rest.

She had made them sit and drink black coffee while she bullied him to bed. Kevin felt great by now and still wanted some action. The walk to the car, the concentration on driving and the coffee had revived him. While the old girl was out of the kitchen, he suggested they go poofter-bashing for a bit of sport. And it was on for the night. As soon as they could get away from the old girl they would head straight for the park. Kevin downed his coffee in a single swallow. He didn't want to waste any more time.

They cruised down the side of the park and past the bog the first time. It didn't look too promising but it was worth a second try. Kevin thought he saw a figure moving between the trees, but it was on its own and miles from the dunnies. You couldn't tell if the cars there were parked for the bog or not. They were too drunk to count them to see if there were any new arrivals the second time around.

The car lurched onto the main road to do another circuit. In the mirror Kevin could see a set of lights crawling slowly behind them past the bog. He thought they were drawing to a stop. It was hard to tell for sure as he'd only seen them just as he'd swung out into the main road. The lights seemed to fade.

"Got one," yelled his mate, pointing back.

"Don't know," mumbled Kevin.

"Give it another try?"

Back round the block. This time they crawled along the edge of the park. It was pretty dark; the trees were quite a way in, the toilets only a dozen yards or so in from the road. The lights inside had been broken. That, or some poof collected them.

Ahead they could see a figure walking along on the same side of the road.

"Cut the lights. Pull over," his mate urged.

The lights dimmed and the car pulled over. They sat staring ahead at the lone pedestrian. He looked back over his shoulder. He must have been aware of the car and that it had stopped somewhere behind him. His look questioned the driver's motives. Friend or foe? it asked in a glance.

"Get down," Kevin ordered. "Better chance if he thinks it's just one of us."

The figure continued to walk but glanced back again. It was hard to see him in the dark but he looked fairly young – tight jeans and a short jacket. The poof looked back again and decided it was alright. He walked slowly across the road at a diagonal, using it as an excuse to look back at the darkened car in an assessing stare. You could see him fairly well for a few seconds as he crossed under one of the lights. He could have avoided it, so he obviously wanted to be seen. They got their look at him. He was young, sure enough, and a little uneasy – just what they were after. Twitchy, you might say, but not going to give up.

"Yep, we've got one."

Kevin was sure this time. He leered back out of the window. "Thinks he's got it made."

His mate was laughing by now.

"Yep, I really fancy this one," Kevin smart-talked.

"Jeez, shut up will you or I'll piss myself down here."

"Stay put," Kevin ordered.

He switched on the parking lights and started the engine. Their quarry turned at the soft noise but kept walking towards the dunnies. The car cruised slowly up trailing him, then pulled over again in the shadows between the sparse street lighting. It was pretty dark. You couldn't tell if there was anyone else around. It looked safe enough.

"I'll get him when he comes out. You stay put."

It was unfair on his mate that Kevin should be having all the say. Usually they acted together; tonight Kevin was hogging it.

"Next one's mine, mate," reckoned his friend.

"Yeah, next one."

The young guy turned into the toilet block, disappearing from sight. He didn't bother to look back one last time.

"Ripper."

And Kevin was out of the car and across the road in a flash. It was a bit of a fucking letdown for his mate. He got up off the floor and stared over the dashboard. He was dying for a piss but it would have to wait now. He could use the bog after Kevin had finished. He could see him in the dark bushes that screened the toilets from the park.

Any minute now he'll get the cunt. But Kevin seemed a bit far off for his mate's liking. Shit, he would probably blow it and they would have to wait to set up the next.

"Next one's mine," he grumbled to himself.

Kevin was standing out clearly, he wasn't trying to

hide. He was waiting for the figure to re-emerge. He'd call the poof over to him for sure. They'd done it before. Kevin would stand there looking at them and just unzip his fly, resting his hand on his tool. They always came running after a fat prick and Kevin always reckoned he had that to show.

In the dim light from the street he could see the figure come out of the bog and look around. He must have been looking for Kevin. No one else inside to pull off.

Kevin strode out of the bushes and beckoned the guy over. He went towards him.

"He's got him," Kevin's mate chortled to himself, and leant over behind the steering wheel for a better look.

The two figures were almost together and he could see that Kevin was bracing himself ready for the big whammo. Nothing unfair, no iron bars or tyre levers, just bare fists. Kevin's mate was still pretty pissed but he didn't want to miss much. He moved across the seat just a little more to see through the side window, and his elbow caught the horn. It was only a short muffled blast but they all heard it.

Like lightning the poof saw the figure in the car and knew what was up. Kevin slugged but only winged the bastard. There was a shout and the guy scrabbled off back towards the bog. Stupid bastard, Kevin would get him in there easy. Lay him out in the dark.

As the young man stumbled back into the toilet block, obscure figures jumped apart, retreating defensively into darker corners and cubicles. The young man scrabbled towards the wall opposite the doorway and groaned. Figures moved in the shadows. Then there was Kevin charging through the door. He was still yelling:

"Come and get it, you bastard."

He skidded to a halt, blinded by the dark. He stared into blackness, his eyes unable to focus. A figure moved behind him. He swung round.

"There you are, you cunt."

The young man clung to the damp wall of the urinal and

said nothing.

Figures moved in the shadows. Kevin could hear them breathing, watching. He stood stock still. Vague shapes began to loom up around him, timid and inquiring, like jungle apes investigating a strange object suddenly in their midst.

"Shit, how many of you bastards are there?" And he lashed out towards the amorphous shapes. There was a thud. He had made contact. A figure stumbled back in the darkness. Then new figures moved in.

He felt hands reach out to touch him. It was eerie, like the blind identifying an object by touch alone. They didn't seem to fear him at all. He was an alien and must be known. Then he felt the figures drawing back. No word had been spoken. He waited.

There was a sharp crack behind him. He swung around. A solid figure blocked the door.

"You fucking poofter!" he screamed.

Another quick movement behind him and still he couldn't see properly.

A cigarette lighter flashed its fire for a moment. It was held high. For a second faces were illuminated around him, then darkness. In the flash of light it was like a witches' coven. Faces illuminated against dank walls . . . male heads, eyes staring, like ancient cave paintings. Then darkness again. The unity was primeval.

Stillness, blackness; he waited.

Suddenly the silence was broken by the crack of an arm across his face. It was a crashing blow, throwing his head sideways. He caught the dark smell of leather. He lurched backwards. Nothing. He waited.

He heard an intake of breath and something crashed down on his skull. He reeled forward to meet a knee butting into his groin. There were sounds of movement everywhere. He lost his nerve. He screamed. A blow smashed into the side of his face and another into his groin. He was sinking fast. He was on his knees, his arms cradling his head. The warm smell of semen greeted him from the ground.

A boot slammed into his back. He jerked out involuntarily. A boot slammed into his groin and he doubled forward again, his hands flung out above his head. Sounds stopped around him. He tried to move, preparing in the dark for the next blow. If he could only get to the protection of one of the corners. He dragged his way along the floor. His hand reached up the dampness of a wall. He felt someone's leg still and quiet. He let go and waited. The blow came. His head crashed to the cement. The smell of deodorant balls and urine; the taste of blood in his mouth.

His mate was getting bored in the car. He'd heard the poof scream once or twice. Kevin must be doing a good job this time. He was still dying for a piss. What the fuck was Kevin up to? He couldn't hold on any longer.

Swinging open the car door, he hauled himself out to piss in the gutter. He was still pretty drunk because he pissed uphill. It ran back on his boots. He swung round to face downhill, spraying the side of the car as he did so.

He was still fumbling with his zip when he saw the first figure coming out of the bog. He expected it to be Kevin. It wasn't. Something was wrong. Then out comes another figure and another. One could have been the poof Kevin chased in; they all looked alike in the dark.

Groping for the open door, he bundled back into the car and pushed down the locks, watching. If something was wrong he wasn't going to be in on it. Kevin would be alright – just a bunch of poofs. Jeez, but how many of them had there been? All these dark shapes just pissing off into the trees.

A figure got into one of the cars parked ahead. He heard a motor bike starting up and he dropped down onto the seat of the car. Another car started up and pulled away. He hid from the lights. He didn't want to be part of it. It was Kevin's idea.

The keys were still in the ignition. Carefully he slid over to the driver's seat. He would just idle the car down to the end of the street in the darkness and then get the hell out of it. But what if the bastards heard him? Better stay there. He cringed back onto the floor and waited. Minutes passed – perhaps five, he couldn't tell.

Kevin would be alright. He could look after himself. He'd scared all the poofs out like rabbits bolting the warren. But he was sure taking his time.

He sat up a little and peered round. No one about. He started the car up and cruised a few yards closer to the bog. The engine running, he gave a few blasts on the horn and waited. What the fuck? Kevin was trying to give him the creeps. What could a bunch of poofs do? Another blast on the horn. Nothing. He switched off the engine and got out of the car. He stood there on the road, then headed for the bog.

Sometimes Kevin could give you the shits when he put the wind up you like this.

No point in waiting any longer. He strode over. Get Kevin at his own game. He crunched over the gravel, then growled in an assumed voice: "Police here, stay where you are."

He sprang through the door.

"Got you, you bastard," he yelled.

Shit, it was so dark, he couldn't see a thing. It was quiet too. He edged carefully forward. There was no one there. His foot hit something. He bent down and felt it. It was a fucking corpse.

One

When the alarm went off, Arthur stayed put. He wasn't going to get out of bed again, ever. Life outside had become quite meaningless and nightmarish. In bed it was warm, safe and comfortable.

He remained deep under the blankets, only the top of his bald head and an aged eye peeping out. At sixty-eight he was too old. The arthritic bend of his back and the permanent droop of his shoulders gave him a foetal look even in everyday life. In bed it was emphasised. An embryo curled up inside the womb putting off the moment of birth.

The alarm had stopped ringing by now. He could hear clattering through in the rest of the house. It had little to do with him. His room was his fortress.

His eye roamed cautiously around the room, then flickered shut again. The room, the mirror, his own beady eye looking back: he wanted to block it all out. Dignity; somewhere along the line he had lost his dignity. The beautiful head of his youth had been transformed into this wizened parrot-like skull. The crowning glory of hair now sat on a styberfoam wigstand by the bed. Life, age; it could make you cry.

Arthur put his head back under the covers to escape from it all. It had happened so quickly without him noticing. One day he had woken up an old man.

He tried to doze a little. Perhaps he did, he couldn't tell. Life had changed so much it played tricks on him. He felt like Rip Van Winkle. Fifty years on and he was back living with Frieda in his mother's house. Those fifty years of almost escaping and never quite making it. Always being brought back to the family in some form. Now Frieda was all the family he had left and still they were together.

He had never liked his sister. After sixty years it was a little late to tell her. He suspected she knew. They were now a habit, little more. It wasn't worth the upset, the violent uprooting, to try to escape now. Escape to what?

All those years of cringing from violence and last night the boy had died before his eyes. Such a different boy than Arthur had been in his youth, but a young life nevertheless. Now the boy would never wake up to find he was sixty-eight and life had passed by in the night, as it had for Arthur.

"You know what they used to call me?" he said to himself. "Golden Boy, they called me Golden Boy."

It still amused him. All those years ago. They were all gone now. Only Arthur, a self-parody, remained. Golden Boy!

He remembered Golden Boy sitting in a restaurant being dined by candle light, his Gary Cooper lookalike sitting opposite. He remembered the carafe of wine, the linen napkins, the discreet smiles, the starched white cuff of his shirt showing below the sleeve of his navy blue suit, as he carefully placed his knife and fork to reach for his wine glass. The care he had taken with himself that night.

Boys dressed to be taken out in his day. Suit, white shirt, tie, hat. He never as much as left the house without his hat. That night he had scrubbed himself for hours, occupying the boarding-house's sole bathroom to the distress of others until he felt he was perfect.

His mind roamed back to the dinner. Nine o'clock, no more wine. Two men leaving the restaurant. Walking through the streets, overcoats over their arms. The rap of feet on the pavement past the lights of the Bourke Street theatres. A few women, who shouldn't have been, loitered on the footpath at the top end of Bourke Street. Going home alone on the tram. The doors opening and closing with each stop. More romance in your head than possible in your life. Things were so difficult, yet the memories so pleasant.

Boasting at the coffee house to the other boys. Long rows of listening faces at "Tates". Sly grog in their satchels. Golden Boy the toast all over again. Always a new lover; this one with a car, that one with friends in the country. A politician, a doctor; Golden Boy was wooed, dined, sent flowers. Feeling like Greta Garbo triumphant alone in his room. The boarding-house breathing his secret all around him. The whistle of a lover waiting in the street.

What had happened to that boy? How had he become this old man, balding, hiding under the counterpane in fear of the world? The boy had been all set for the world. He could have conquered it. Now he was a fugitive hiding from his crime beneath pink candlewick.

And when the police came to take him away, Frieda would stand on the footpath wearing her check apron and furry slippers, her head cocked on one side. She would become one of the condemning neighbours. No love lost in their house, their mother's house, as it would forever be known. Frieda like her mother, only now years older. One husband and two children dead and still Frieda nodded and twitched on. He hated her. Every time he looked at her he was reminded of his own age. Why had death been so cruel as to spare both of them so long? If only she would die, he could sell their mother's house and be free.

Frieda would outlive him too. It was Frieda's way. The house would one day be hers alone and she would stay in it, letting it crumble around her to deprive other generations.

Arthur would stay in bed. His mind was resolved. He didn't want to face whistling kettles and cold toast in the kitchen. He would stay where he was and think it out. He turned over in bed and faced the wall.

What had happened the night before? Where had he gone so wrong? Had he really been part of it? Arthur, who had left the army ignominiously because all he could do was work in the officers' mess and dance the girl's part at the parties in the hut. Arthur the pansy. They had made his life hell on the parade ground. He had collapsed, been discharged and back in Melbourne doing the beats all within a year.

Arthur, who couldn't even look at blood without feeling faint – had he been part and parcel to the beating down of that young thug in the park? He couldn't comprehend it. He had never had a violent bone in his body.

At least Ronnie was not alive to know.

It was after the war he had first met Ronnie. He had seen him for the last time – when? About ten years ago. Arthur's mother had died. Ronnie had sent flowers and a letter. The letter had said, "Now you can come and live with me."

Poor Ronnie had never given up. Time after time if Arthur's life was in a mess, he would turn up and make the same offer:

"Come and stay with me Arthur. It won't matter what others say – at least it won't matter to me."

Arthur had known too late that he loved Ronnie. It had taken a drunken driver and a hit-and-run, to prove that Ronnie had needed him too. Just an old man too slow crossing the road. They didn't even call it manslaughter. All his life Arthur had been alone. Only on Ronnie's death had he known that he missed out on something he had always wanted.

Some drunken driver, like the thug in the park. Perhaps that was it, perhaps it had been revenge that had made Arthur strike back? All those years Ronnie had loved Arthur, long after he had ceased to be Golden Boy. Arthur must have been thirty when they met. Ronnie was the first lover he'd had of his own age. Always he had gone for older men. It was part of life in the Depression. Only an older man could afford to take you out. Young boys just went out together as a group of queens, not on what they later called dating. "Dating" and "cocksucker": the only terms the Yanks had left with them.

Such a violent death for a young boy.

Arthur remembered a fight one night at the Hotel Australia. It had been in the downstairs bar. It was pretty infamous to be seen there; you didn't go if you had a reputation to lose. Then one night rumour had it the Duke of Edinburgh had walked in. The old Stud Pit had buzzed for weeks after that. But Arthur remembered the night there had been a fight there. A couple of army guys had tried to ram a broken glass into some camp guy's face. He was supposed to have propositioned them. Everyone knew he hadn't. They had shoved the guy up against the wall with the jagged end of the glass inches from his throat. He had squawked out in horror. Suddenly the place had been full of screaming queens all fighting to get out of the place, protecting their faces and their names.

It was the first time Arthur could recall seeing straights going out of their way to bash up queers. Poofter, they had called the guy. The word still reeked of the insult to this day. Poofter, camp. Mein Kampf – my struggle, long before it was Adolf Hitler's.

But in those days, out in the open, the parks and beats had been safe. The patrols went through but they couldn't keep up with the numbers, so you were safe. St Kilda Road had been a sight to the eyes. Flinder's Street up to the Shrine – you could see them swinging their hips along, offering and finding anything you could imagine. No matter how much people said things had progressed, there wasn't anything you could do now that they didn't do in those days too. The bushes in the gardens had been alive, yet no one seemed to get hurt.

Arthur remembered an enormous negro he had picked up one night off one of the Yank ships. They had met at the beat on the corner of Toorak Road. It was gone now, filled in by the council one night. The sailor had looked like King Kong in the half-light but was as gentle as a baby in the bushes of the Alexander Gardens. He had made Arthur promise to come back and meet him the next night, called him "my white princess". Of course Arthur hadn't gone back. You couldn't be seen with a negro by the other Yanks. He told the other queens about it though. The giant penis story was kept alive for years but Arthur never told them how the guy kissed his hand as they parted under the lights of Prince's Bridge.

That's what sex in the park had meant to them during the war. Things had changed. Arthur couldn't understand why. Where had all this anger come from?

What could lead a young guy to go out specifically to thump up queens? What had led them to thumping back? Arthur didn't understand anything anymore.

He heard a noise at the door, then it opened. Frieda stood there looking startled as ever. She's come to make sure I'm not dead, he thought.

"Aren't you getting up lazybones, uh?" she asked.

He shrugged his head and turned over.

"Suit yourself," she said and shuffled out again.

"Old pussy," she mumbled to herself.

But she was grateful. Glad he wasn't dead, glad not to be alone. Arthur had always been his mother's boy; now he was hers. It was as if her own family had been only coincidental to her life. A period of time occupied until summoned back again to her mother's house. Now there was only Arthur to care for and her job in life would be complete. He was still a child with his vanity, his false hair and those secret night excursions. She couldn't leave Arthur alone, she would have to be there until the end. It wouldn't be right, a man alone.

Arthur heard what she mumbled as she shut the door. An old pussy was he now? Stupid old goat, what would she know? She couldn't even look after herself. Frieda had never been close, they'd never been able to talk like he could with some women. The movies were just a waste of money to her. She had thought Joseph Cotton looked like the man in the hardware shop near the market. They probably did look alike by now. Old men and corpses all look alike. And Golden Boy started to cry. He didn't want to end his days in prison.

Frieda returned clattering noisily at the door. She bore an old wicker breakfast tray. She forced him to sit up while she plumped up the pillows behind him, then placed the tray on his chest. It was too awkward for him to reach.

She muttered something and fumbled her way out again.

"Just leave me alone, do you hear," he shouted at the closing door. She made no reply.

"Poor old fool's been crying," she thought to herself. He was the only man she had ever seen cry – except at funerals, that was. She'd seen it before, like when that funny old friend Ronnie had come round for the last time after mother had died. He hadn't cried at his mother's funeral but he had shut himself in his room and cried after Ronnie had left.

And there was another time too. They had heard over the radio that Ronnie had been run over – dead. It was such a shock hearing it over the air like he was a celebrity or something. The shock had really got to Arthur. It was as if he had never really recovered even now.

Arthur looked over the top of the tray and stared blindly at the dressing-table mirror beyond. He could feel the slow teardrops moving down the furrows in his face. They moved silently, but occasionally the crockery rattled on the tray before him as his chest jerked slightly up and down.

The ginger toupee on its wigblock shone synthetically from the dressing-table. He tried to focus on the mirror but could see only an old man looking questioningly back.

There was another wig he had worn once years ago when Golden Boy had made his debut at the club. Bridge club by day, cabaret by night. Drag had been very big then, they had all done it. Arriving at the club and changing there, emerging like swans from the dressing-rooms to sit coyly at their own tables, only mixing with those you knew or were introduced to. Meetings were set up formally in those days, none of your casual fraternising. Then once a year, the debs' night. He had made his coming out there like all the others. Dressed all in white, gloves, trains, more feathers than in a mattress factory. And the wig. Curls of gold. Guided down the steps to a man stiff and formal in evening dress. There had been glamour in those days and it was all so nearly in his reach.

Now by day he wore his cheap wig, his plastic teeth and

the grey flannel trousers of old age. The crotch met at his knees and the waistband was as large as his chest. These days he looked deformed with his clothes off. From behind, his bottom had completely disappeared. It was only from the front that you could see it had retreated into his body to come out on the other side in the form of a hard ball-like stomach. It hid his feet and dwarfed his genitals. Only by the dishonesty of night did it tempt anyone into activity.

He still did the beats but these days it was mainly as a voyeur. Few men showed interest in someone of his age and when they did, his capacity sometimes let him down. It was time to admit that he found it hard to sustain an erection. Erection – the word made him blush. At sixty-eight it was hard enough to get one at all, let alone keep it up for hours while people dallied and made up their mind. His best hope these days was to take his teeth out and do what the Americans liked best. All the Yanks he had known and that was all they ever wanted to do. Cocksucking Yanks. Even McCarthy hadn't been able to keep them from that.

A whole history of repression, that was his life. He looked down at his body. He remembered when it had been so good he had paraded it at the swimming baths.

The City Baths. Men Only in those days and of course at all the baths it was nude swimming. They had ruined it letting the women in and going mixed. It had eventually closed the City Baths. Nice to know they had reopened them now and that they were cruisy all over again. All those male bodies and he had strutted with the best.

Eyes meeting eyes. Splashing around, touching underwater. Outswimming each other. Following eyes watching chests, buttocks. Men too excited to get out of the water. Then two strangers managing to arrive in the changing-room at the same time. Those furtive trips to the communal showers. Only two showers – how could you avoid making physical contact? Discretion, and you would never make a mistake.

He remembered well one such encounter that had

started under the showers at the baths. They had gone for a drive along the Yarra, leaving the car at Studley Park. On foot they had walked a long way down the bank, and there beneath the summer night's sky had made love on a blanket.

In the showers he had thought the guy like Johnny Weismuller; in the moonlight he could see he was Adonis. They had walked back to the parked car, hand in hand through the darkness. He had found the next day his clothes were all marked from the grass. He had been back to the baths again and again but such nights are not repeatable. He had made love to a god on a blanket by the river and for that night Golden Boy had been a god too.

He heard the side door shut as Frieda left on her Saturday morning ritual. The TAB betting office must be open already. He manoeuvred higher up the bed and tested the teapot with his fingertips. The tea was cold. He tried to move. The teapot rattled awkwardly, then remained still. Grasping the sides of the tray, he twisted his body round and swung his legs out of bed. Nothing had spilt. He sat stupidly for a moment on the edge of the bed still holding the tray. He then stooped forward and slid it onto the floor. The crockery clattered dangerously. Arthur watched with interest until all movement stopped. True to his earlier vow he then again clawed his way low beneath the covers, retreating into their safety like an injured possum into the protection of its tree.

He wasn't going to get up until everything was clear in his mind. All rationale had deserted the crazy world out there and he wasn't going to join it. In the cold moonlight of a suburban park he had been forced into commando action. Kill or be killed; maim or be maimed. The world had gone mad. A thug had come to bash and destroy and had himself been bashed and destroyed. The justice that far was plain; but that Arthur, at his age, had beaten to death a young man in his prime of youth, was as unpalatable as it was improbable. Queens and straights were not at war, so why had he and the others killed with little motive and no compunction? It was an ignoble end to anyone's life. What of Golden Boy? Had Arthur beaten him to death too in one and the same action?

He hadn't wanted to kill anyone, ever.

Sinking lower into the protection of his bed, Arthur closed his mind to this and all other thoughts. He drifted into a fitful sleep where his body was at rest and his mind tormented and active.

He saw himself and Ronnie both resplendent in evening dress, descending the stairs into the foyer of the Regent Theatre. The performance was over; they were the first to leave as a crowd surged behind them. In the background the applause still resounded for a final curtain call. Ushers stood back, a guard of honour to the passing patrons. Ronnie was beside him. An odd thing, he felt Ronnie's hand lightly on his back guiding him down the stairs. The physical contact in public was both exhilarating and a trifle embarrassing. He knew the warmth of what it said, feared the cut of what others would say.

Ronnie's hand on his back, then things became a blur. At the foot of the steps lights shone upwards into their faces. A new noise greeted them from below. Figures in uniform waiting. There was some kind of scuffle around him. He couldn't see Ronnie. The damn lights blinded him. Ronnie's hand trying to rush him on one way. Arms reaching out to drag him another. Crowds surged down the stairs all around, confusing him. He lost Ronnie. Hordes of well dressed patrons clamoured between them. He stumbled forward alone. A strong grip on his arm, something at each wrist and he couldn't pull his hands apart. The lights flashed. Cameras behind them clicked and he was being led away. Ronnie, pushed to the ground, was held there helpless as Arthur was led away by the police.

He started awake, springing up and gazing disoriented at the room around him. The familiar blue and white curtains were lit by the early afternoon sun. He brought his hands to his temples and gazed around. He was alright, his hands told him; bald, but alright. He dropped his hands to rest on the agitated bedclothes over his body. He gasped for reality, groping in the void.

A familiar sound came to his ears, reassuring in its normality. Frieda was listening to the races on the wireless in the kitchen.

As long as she could remember she had always had the races. Pity that today they interrupted the broadcast with a news flash about identifying some dead boy. She didn't catch whether it was a boating or a car accident. Car, she decided. People didn't drown like they used to.

She poured herself another cup of tea. Arthur would be asleep. It was as well to leave him alone. Nature was the best cure, that was her philosophy.

Arthur lay in bed listening to the high-pitched call of the races from the back room. It had never interested him much. He'd never got into the Members' Stand and considered it degrading to be in the outer. For a period – when was it? Oh, twenty years back, maybe thirty – he had gone to the wrestling a few times with a friend. He liked watching the bodies cavorting about but had to be continually reassured that no one was really being hurt. It was alright as long as none of it was real, like in the movies. You could see that the punches always missed in the movies and Arthur liked it that way. If only last night had been a charade like that too. But he had a feeling that once he left that bed, he would know it was all real.

The afternoon slowly passed. The light changed, the noises outside altered. The day was passing by. He was going to have to leave the bed soon.

Finally, late in the afternoon, his bladder won out and he had to sneak along the passage to the bathroom. With any luck Frieda would be too engrossed in Moonee Valley to hear him. He stood peeing far back into the bowl so it hit the porcelain and made less noise as it trickled down into the bowl. He cringed at the noise of the flushing and crept back along the passageway using the wall for support.

When he returned to his room, he realised his breakfast tray had gone. He tried to remember if it had been there when he left. He couldn't be sure. He got back into bed anyway.

That was one thing about Frieda, she would move around quietly and pry where she had no call to. She knew not to tidy his room but couldn't keep herself out of it. Sometimes he felt like planting one of those magazines under his mattress just to shock her. Young men nude in army boots, escort services, that sort of thing. He chuckled, he couldn't help himself; but he wouldn't do it.

Things had all become so much more blatant. Arthur couldn't understand how the whole thing had started. One day he had picked up a newspaper and there it was, male-to-male sex as close as a phone call away. Dreams, fantasies realised for the exchange of cash. Somehow it didn't seem right, sex as a business transaction. There had been few commercial guys around in his memory. Oh you heard a rumour or two around the pubs – someone had made an offer, someone else had accepted – but that was all. In his youth it had been a young man's prerogative to receive presents – clothes, outings, food even – but not hard cash.

How could you pick up a phone and order what you wanted? It was so impersonal. Until you saw the boy you wouldn't know what you wanted. You might not want anything at all.

Even through the Depression he couldn't recall any commercial guys. Young people today had no romance, just price tags. The gays were as bad as the straights. He just couldn't figure how things had gone so wrong. The beats had always provided free sex. He had always believed it was degrading to pay for it. He couldn't change now, although he knew many of his vintage had. It wasn't for him.

He remembered the sheath of gladioli and was glad that Golden Boy had been wooed that way instead. The poor creatures today were missing so much. Their time was money. To him time had been romance.

The nights of going to the theatre with some handsome man. The plays, the musicals, the Tiv. Until he met Ronnie, his dates had never had the courage to sit with him. They had always had separate tickets, seeing each other only after the show for a discreet supper. With Ronnie they had sat brazenly together. No need for the cover of two of the lesbian girls he knew from the coffee houses, not with Ronnie. Ronnie had been very modern thinking. Arthur had always held back.

He had been so embarrassed the night they had stayed at the Melbourne. Everyone there was gay. The place only had about eight rooms for accommodation, but Arthur couldn't face the reception desk the way Ronnie had. They had been so excited spending the whole night together they hadn't got around to having sex. It had been so, so romantic.

They should have lived together at the end. After his mother's death there should have been a time. But the end had come so suddenly.

It was after Ronnie's death that Arthur had started to do the beats again. It was the second time in his life. The first time around he had been young, pretty and in demand. This last time he had known the rejection, the desperation and the loneliness of spending old age alone.

At first it had been hard even to find them, things had changed so much. Many had been lost or destroyed. The Trak had been buried and the last wreath laid years before. He tried the Town Hall. It was closed. He tried the Post Office. It was now attended.

The Lobster Pot still stood in its Victorian splendour, but judging by his sojourn there, nothing had been caught there for years. Further out of town things had changed too. The dear old St George's Road had been demolished completely. The Spanish Mission was still open but it was all rent, louts and drugs. The whole scene was suddenly more violent.

Then Arthur had found this new gem, a jewel amongst jewels and so handy. It had served his voyeur's needs well. He often went lookout for other couples or mutely watched their sexual gymnastics from the safe distance of the toilet throne. He was not averse to giving the odd blow job, with his teeth out. But there was a problem. His toupee was very detectable from the vantage point offered by oral sex. He lived in fear some bitchy queen would one day remove it for all to see.

These last years of watching hadn't been so bad. He made friends, younger men. They got to recognise his face, nod, smile, make him feel part of the communal side of it. Many spoke to him, sat in the park to swop a few words, share a joke or gossip. He wanted little more. He was capable of little more. He couldn't regain his chance with Ronnie but he was accepted and that Ronnie would have been proud of.

He thought of his ventures into the beats in the heyday during the war and before. He remembered the toilets behind Luna Park. It seemed as many flocked there as to the funfair itself. True, the sex there was quick, anonymous, but hardly furtive. Walking through the bushes was a revelation. Heads and bums popping up all over the place, just to resubmerge when they could see it was all safe.

On a busy night Arthur couldn't remember who, how many or even what. And you never met any trouble there. Not one bad experience could Arthur recall. Not one. Yet the area was full of straights from Luna Park and the coffee shops of Acland Street, crowds from the theatre and stray sailors from the ships, maurading the shore for sex like the pirates of old. More than one sailor had found his way to the Peanut Farm and not just for a piss either. There had never been any trouble in those days. It had all been accepted. Nothing like last night had ever occurred.

His line of thought was broken by Frieda fumbling at the door.

"No Frieda, I'm not dead," he hollered at the moving door.

She chose to ignore the remark. Either that or her growing deafness had muffled the meaning. She pushed the door wide and stood there, head cocked on one side, her gaze depriving him of any last vestige of privacy.

"Feeling crook, are we?" she asked.

He tried to regain his dignity and in his most correct

manner announced, "A little tired, that's all."

"I'll make some tea. But I'm not bringing it in here."

He hesitated and shook his head. Her head twitched with impatience. "Bloody hypochondriac."

She turned and nosed her way rodent-like back along the passage towards the warm den of the kitchen.

He waited several minutes. He heard the whistle of the kettle screaming its urgency into the stillness of the house. Frieda was slow getting up to turn it off. It would let him know it was ready.

Reluctantly he got out of bed and struggled into the dressing-gown from the chair beside the bed. He looked resignedly in the mirror. It was an old man in an old man's check dressing-gown he saw. Stubbornly he took the wig from its other head and placed it doormat-like on his own. It needed brushing.

For Frieda's sake he put his teeth in. He stood at the door and mimicked to the mirror, "Bloody hypochondriac."

"There you are," she announced.

He didn't bother to reply. He sat on his chair and watched her pouring the tea. It was country tea, strong and brewed, splashing into the cups in a rust brown stream.

"Drink up," she advised.

He watched her pour her precious "top of the milk" in last, then pass his cup over. There hadn't been any cream to skim off for years, not since pasteurization. He was glad. He had always hated the greasy globules that resulted when the cream was added to hot tea.

"Did well on the horses," she said.

He wasn't interested. She looked over at him. Maybe he was really crook after all. He looked very pale sitting there, but then Arthur had always been one for melodramas. Spent too much time in the movies. Last night she had been in bed before he got home. Out that late, it was no wonder he caught a chill.

"You shouldn't go to the pictures so late." She looked over to him.

"What?"

"You shouldn't stay out all hours going to the pictures," she repeated.

So that was what she thought. The nights he spent hunting the streets in his loneliness, she thought he spent at the cinema. He hardly ever went to see films these days. All his stars were too old now. If they did make an appearance at all it was as little old ladies or drunks. No glamour. He'd seen that last movie Henry Fonda had made. You wouldn't look twice at the man now and how they had all envied him once. It just made him depressed.

He took a sip of tea.

"I knew you would come round," Frieda announced triumphantly.

It was good to see him coming back to normal. He'd got bad at brooding of late. He missed his mates but what could she do, they were all dead. It was alright for a woman. She still had the house to run, but growing old was tougher on a man. Once he lost his mates he had nothing.

She started to set the table. He sat on. Unfolding the lace cloth, she studied it for wear. It was one Arthur had given her during the war. That was what he had been like in those days. Call in to see her, a couple of linen table-cloths, a half bottle of brandy for Alf. No one asked where it came from. The girls had always liked Arthur, though Alf had been a little hard about him at times. Any unmarried man was a poofter to him. Such language wasn't permissible about family. People should keep thoughts like that to themselves.

She switched on the telly. It would be good for Arthur to sit up for a bit. She went through to the kitchen. The television played for itself.

He just wanted to sit there in the warm and think the whole thing through. Decide what to do. Say nothing? Go to the police? Wait for them to come to him? How could they justify what they had done to a young boy in the cold evening of the park? Why had he attacked them? If he hadn't charged in the way he did, nothing would have happened. He could have just walked by and left the lot of them alone. He could still be alive today. What had they done to him to warrant such anger and loathing?

And the other men. They had acted as Arthur had too. Did they understand any more than he did? Would they keep their conspiracy together? Six strangers all trusting each other. It was all so difficult to understand. Even during the war, when life meant so little to the politicians, it had meant more to them than it had last night.

The television screen flickered in front of him but he took no notice. The picture had been bad for weeks.

He still worried at the events in the park but could find no solution. After last night, he wouldn't be able to do the beats without fear. Again he thought of the ease of the old days when the beats belonged to the camp guys and the straights left them all well alone. Captain Cook's Cottage had been as safe by night as a drink at the Menzies.

The Menzies. God, he had forgotten about the place. A sad day they pulled that down. The cream had drunk at the Menzies and he had been there with them. The Menzies at its height. That was a memory.

He had first met Ronnie at the Menzies. People didn't normally meet there for the first time, but Ronnie had been more forward than most. The Menzies had always been very discreet. With six o'clock closing, you only had time to meet friends and decide where to go next. But he had first met Ronnie there. Today you would call it being picked up. Ronnie had simply come up, introduced himself and waited. All the other queens were appalled but he and Arthur went off to "Bill's" together and that was the beginning of that.

Frieda's head appeared. She looked around and said, "You're not watching the news."

She trotted forward and aggressively yanked the knob of the set around several stations. She was such a brutal creature when it came to inanimate objects. Arthur felt repelled by her violence at times. Yet he couldn't imagine her beating another human being to death in the park. He couldn't try to tell her what had happened. She wouldn't understand any of it. It was best if he just held it inside until he sorted it out.

The television played through its news broadcast. Arthur ignored it. Frieda banged around uninhibitedly in the kitchen. And Arthur longed to be Golden Boy again. To be back in the past where he really belonged.

Ronnie had always said you had to move with the times but Arthur didn't want to. He was an old man, the mirror told him so. His youth, his hope, was all in the past. It could only be relived by looking back. He didn't fit in this modern world. It hadn't been him in the park at all. This news broadcast, it didn't mean anything to him. Arabs were men who abducted women on white horses and Ronald Reagan was a movie star. All this stuff flashing before him meant nothing.

Ronnie had always said he should be more interested in politics but it wasn't his nature. Ronnie had been the one who wanted to change the world. He would have been pleased about the new laws, pleased about the bars, all of it. If only he had been here to enjoy it.

For the second time that day he started to cry. He sobbed audibly. Freida heard it from the next room. She arrived in the doorway wiping her hands on her apron and looking bewildered.

She looked at the flickering newsreader on the television. He was midway through something about giving out the name of that dead boy. She still hadn't caught what had happened to him and here was her own brother, a grown man, crying like a baby.

"You feeling sick?" she asked.

He shook his head and continued to sob. He looked awful.

"Was it the News?" she asked. "I'll switch it off?"

He beckoned her to him and she went. She stood holding his head as he cried into her old bosom. Boys died all the time, it wasn't that bad. In the war they had got used to it.

Slowly his sobbing subsided and the convulsions stopped. For a long time she stood there holding him. It felt good. No one had needed her like that for years and it felt good to be there with Arthur needing her so much.

"There, there," she crooned in her soft old voice.

It comforted and reassured them both.

Finally he separated himself and sat upright again. Still the television danced its flickering image into the room.

It was their room, their home, just as it had been their mother's before them. Frieda would preserve this home just as long as there was anyone there to need it.

"It's alright now," Arthur mumbled and she knew it was her cue to go. He would be embarrassed her seeing him cry like that. She returned to the kitchen.

Arthur shook a little to himself in his comfortless chair. He spoke aloud the thought that filled his head.

"I want Ronnie," he said.

"I want Ronnie, he would understand."

Two

When Gerry got to work on Monday, Sue was already ensconced at her desk. He noted she had signed on at eight. She was reading a magazine but slid it into her drawer when she saw him coming. He'd caught sight of it though, another copy of *Bride*. Sometimes he despaired of the girl. With this new affirmative action plan, in a few months his job could have been hers. It had taken him years to get there. Instead of taking advantage of the scheme, she had to be watched all the time. He just couldn't get through to her.

All her thoughts were on the wedding; she was too busy to think about her job. Her quotas were a mess and he always had to help her out at the end of the day. She was, of course, always happy to do overtime to catch up. With the cost of the wedding it was almost essential to her; but it shouldn't be necessary, that was the point.

Gerry always tried to be patient to preserve a good working relationship because in the past people had made it so hard for him when he first started. Seeing her today with the magazine was nearly too much. He suppressed the feeling of nausea that rose from his stomach. The prospect of confrontation on today of all days.

He was apprehensive about the incident with the boy. He had scanned every paper in sight for some news. The late news Saturday had played it down. By this morning there had been an appeal to the public for information. Gerry was now worried precisely because he had that information. In addition there was his concern about Robert. Then this morning there was Sue calmly reading *Bride* for her own rosy future and placing him in a position of having to admonish her. It was all so petty in comparison. He wanted to point at the half-hidden magazine and shout like a small boy:

"I saw."

She would have been quite lost if he had. Instead he went for a more calm approach.

"Found the dress yet?" he asked, placing his bag on his desk. It sounded a little bitchy to him but she didn's seem to notice. She smiled happily and replied, "No. It's so hard. I know what I want but I can't explain it to anyone."

"It's hard," he said, nodding his understanding and sitting down.

A pile of Friday's chits and the chart sat there waiting for him. Bookings were getting dangerously full for the school-holiday period and it was about time to place a countdown on the agents. He'd do it himself. He always ended up taking so much on himself, trying to prove his worth.

She was saying, "I want a tight bodice and a really full skirt."

She was dragging the magazine back out of her desk: "I'll show you. It's nice the way you're interested, most men aren't. Oh Steve is, but then it's his wedding."

He tried to show his disinterest tactfully by organizing his desk to start work. When had he last been to a wedding? Weddings were just part of the world he was precluded from. Just a ritualistic handing over of a woman from one man to another.

"Who gives this woman?"

"I do."

It said it all. He'd have thought women would have wanted to reject it most.

"I like this, only I don't like the neckline and I want real lace."

He glanced politely at the picture she held up.

"Fifties Edith Head," he mumbled.

She looked blank, then said, "It's about $700", as if that in some way justified the choice. "I'll have it made. It's better that way."

"You're going to spend $700 on a wedding dress?" he asked.

"They're all about that price. It's a very expensive business getting married."

"So it would seem."

It really was time to get started on the work piled before them and he didn't want to resort to upsetting her.

"Not being married you probably wouldn't know," she retorted.

He wasn't sure if the malice was intended. Sometimes he thought her brain quite dull, sometimes slyly perceptive.

"You'll get it all back in wedding presents," he replied. "Now hadn't we better start work, dear? I've still got to sort out that 7.45 you took on Thursday – such a pity we don't go to Warrambool at that time."

She was quiet and he felt he had been lousy. It hadn't been necessary to call her dear. It was just that her mind was never on her work these days. Some of her mistakes were awful to sort out. Pauline, from counter bookings, would hang, draw and quarter any of her crew that took such things.

He started to work through the chits in silence. His mind flew back.

They had released the boy's name but nothing more. He was only a boy, twenty, the same age as Sue's fiancé in fact. In the darkness he had seemed older.

He shut off and worked.

Only the last minute telephone chits to do and he was up to date.

Back with Friday night. A dark figure slumping helpless to the ground. He didn't regret it. He felt no remorse. It was just having to keep quiet about it that played on his mind. Like everything else of his private life, at work it must remain private. Repressed into secrecy for twenty years now – or was it more? It was a way of life. His stomach wrenched in his desire to get out.

"I want Steve to wear a dinner suit."

She had stopped work. "It will look better with my

dress. Chesters have some new double-breasted ones."

It was no good, the wedding must take sway. Involuntarily he replied, "Don't you think Steve is a bit short for a double-breaster?"

He had stopped himself saying "thick". Gerry thought of Steve as a stocky little guy, the sort who was only at home in the most casual clothes.

She mused the idea; then: "But it will look so good against my dress."

He put down his pen. "You haven't chosen your dress yet."

She fought back: "But I know what I want."

The same hint of malice was there.

"Let's do some work, shall we?" he said.

She slammed the magazine back into the drawer and noisily thumbed through Friday's sheets.

"I started at eight," she said, "so I'm leaving at four."

She continued to rattle her way through her papers.

If only his problems had been dinner suits. He was dying for morning tea to see if anyone had a later edition of the paper.

Bugger! They had overbooked the 10.30 for the eighth. Another series of phone calls he'd have to make, reeking of apologies and humiliation, all for someone else's error. He looked over to Sue. She was obviously bogged down with her load. It was nearly nine and the rush would start soon.

"Give those to me," he said, "I'll clear them so you can be ready for the calls."

"Thanks," she said.

He wasn't that bad really. Just a bit of an old woman when it came to being up to date. Living alone often seemed to make men fussy, she thought. It must be not having a wife to look after you.

Come ten o'clock, she declined going to tea before him. One of them had to stay and answer the phones. He guessed she had a series of private calls to make and wanted him out of the way to do so. It suited him fine. They all did that. So long as they kept up to date with the bookings, he didn't mind too much.

The tea room wasn't too full. He helped himself to coffee from the urn and picked up a couple of spare papers left lying around. He always sat on his own, or with some of the older women. All the men ignored him.

He scanned the paper. He was in luck. Just an appeal to the gay community for information, an assurance of confidentiality, etc. The other paper carried a photograph of Mrs Schultz and an appeal to go with it. In one breath she disowned her son from anything to do with queers. In the next she appealed to them for help. She went on to say no one who knew Kevin could accuse him of being "like that", he was a "man's man". What an inaccurate phrase, Gerry thought. Surely he was a man's man himself?

The article ended with a demand that the police clean up the parks to avoid this kind of mistake happening again. The problem was not to control the marauding adolescents but preventing the perverts from meeting there. That would solve the problem. In its own way it was logical. You can't go poofter-bashing with no poofters there to bash. It also recommended the closing down of certain pubs and late-night clubs that attracted this undesirable type, hence opening the possibility to further violence in the area.

Gerry was gazing hard at Mrs Schulz and wondering if her son had been as ugly as his mother in both body and mind, when Pauline plumped down beside him. Plumped down she did, big loose mounds of thigh dropping over the small chair. She still wore the short skirts of her youth. On anyone else it would lead to them sitting cautiously, legs together; with Pauline it didn't matter. The giant thighs met in a pool of flesh and indiscretion was impossible.

"How's it going Gerry, love?" she asked. It was a bit how you might speak to your favourite puppy. He was an oddity to her eyes. He surreptitiously closed the paper and prepared for the description of the weekend which he knew was imminent.

To begin, Pauline announced: "I think I'll have to get married again, Gerry, I need the rest. Had a fantastic weekend."

Gerry remembered "fantastic" as a word from his own youth. Now everything was wonderful. Sue would have a wonderful dress and look wonderful on that wonderful special day.

"Sorry Pauline," he replied, "I've told you before I won't marry you."

She looked hard at him, then slapped her thighs laughing. To Gerry she was all thigh. It wobbled as she walked, revealed itself as she bent over and came in for a pounding when she laughed. Yet she was no threat and they got along well.

Connie joined them, fruit cake already in her mouth.

"See in the paper about that pervert in the park." The p's made her spit fruit cake at everyone in general.

"It says in the paper he wasn't a pervert," Gerry replied quietly.

But Connie wasn't interested.

"Picture of his poor mother too. It must have broken her heart him turning out that way. If one of mine did . . ." She paused.

"You could share his dresses," Pauline joined in. And again the thighs were punished for her laughter.

"Line them up and shoot them, that's what I say."

Connie looked around for support. Pauline liked Gerry and had her own ideas about him. Must be hard for him to take it sitting there listening to Connie. Gerry who wouldn't hurt a fly. He'd been taking it for years.

"I think it's alright when it's just between boys, Connie. It's just horseplay. I mean it's not like it was anything real – like rape, I mean."

"Shoot them."

Connie was adamant.

Pauline gave Gerry a raise of her eyebrow to show her own opinion and then prepared to tell them about her weekend of conquests. Pauline knew and didn't know about Gerry. She and Gerry never openly discussed it but she knew what the other men said behind his back. Why he was stuck in the rut of what they called "women's work". His promotion prospects were like her own or Connie's, not like those of the accepted men who got on with their mates. Poor old Gerry.

Not that Gerry didn't work hard, she knew he did, but – well people didn't take him seriously. They suspected he was a bit bent. It was Pauline's own term for Gerry – bent, a bit off the straight and narrow.

"Shoot them all," Connie was repeating to no one in particular.

"Where were you when the Führer called?" Gerry asked.

It didn't register at first. Then Connie gulped her fruit cake in indignation. Her reply was almost comic.

"What? I'll have you know both my husband and father fought the Germans."

That's right, women and children first, apart from when it came to waging war. That was Connie all over.

"Perhaps they didn't know how to change sides," he quipped.

And he left the tea room. Why should he take shit from her anymore?

The rest of the morning passed quickly enough. Sue took her magazine to tea with her and came back with the dour advice from Connie that brides always lose weight before the wedding so you couldn't get your dress made too much beforehand. Connie knew of one girl who had paid and extra $100 because the dress had to be altered the night before and all the beadwork redone. Of course, Connie would.

Pauline had pointed out that many brides she knew put on weight drastically before the wedding – mainly in terms of a swelling stomach and milk-enlarged breasts. That wasn't going to happen to Sue. Steve was prepared to wait. He was a gentleman.

Gerry was wondering if anyone saw him slipping out of the park or his car idling away into the night. The evening stayed in his mind with a queer exhilaration. He had finally struck back. All through the morning this dull thought had been there. Now it found words. At last he had struck back.

He could sit through all the wedding talk, Pauline's talk of her conquests, Connie's principle of the final solution; it all no longer mattered. His own life had always been shoved under the carpet at work. With whom could he share the stories of his infatuations, his loves, his fond memories? For years he had been relegated to some backseat position at work. The middle-aged single man, like a maiden aunt. No one knew of his desires to share his life, to own his own home, to have his own special memories, to celebrate his own special anniversaries. It was considered not nice to have aspirations outside of marriage. Could he tell them of his lover, their strivings and disappointments? Could he pull out a gay guide to the city and discuss his forthcoming weekend, or even discuss it in retrospect? Yet compromising himself so far, he had been overlooked time and time again for promotion. As Connie pointed out, they promote the married men first, it's fairer. Could he then cry to the equal opportunity board?

Not being one of the boys had had its consequences, but it was still legal to discriminate against him on terms of his "sexual tastes". "Sexual taste", such a distasteful word. It sounded as if he was obsessed with oral sex.

He had been pushed back into mediocrity for all these years. At work he was a sexless freak. In society it was alright for him to be denied housing, a joint loan or even joint insurance with his lover. And here was Sue organizing her wedding of the year. No wonder he was bitter. But he had hit back on Friday night.

The thing that both exhilarated and petrified Gerry about Friday night was that he felt no guilt about the boy. Gerry was apprehensive that Robert would find out where he had been. Their relationship was too important for him to have put it at that kind of risk. Ten years they had been together. Had he put those ten years in jeopardy? He regretted being there but not what they had done. The realization made him feel light and crazy in the head.

Sue's phone rang. It was Steve. They always indulged in long personal calls during the day. She was uninhibited now about exchanging terms of affection and did it with a new bravado that he envied. Gerry thought that next time Robert phoned, he too should publicly indulge in all those terms of endearment that had only been whispered in the privacy of their home.

But it was time to blot it out with work as he had done for years. Work killed injustice, for the moment at least.

"Steve's coming up so we can go to lunch early. You don't mind if I go now, do you?"

He wondered why she had asked.

"No, no, I don't mind."

Love wasn't only for the young, it was only for the straight.

Steve sat on the corner of Sue's desk and looked slightly awkward. She had gone to wash her hands, her euphemism for going to the toilet. Gerry thought Steve felt awkward at being left with him. He cleared his throat,

"I haven't congratulated you on your engagement yet," he said.

Steve looked across at him swinging his leg nervously.

"Yeah," he said and looked down.

"Should I?" asked Gerry.

"What?"

"Congratulate you."

Steve laughed, "Yeah."

Gerry leaned back and looked at him. Steve shifted uncomfortably under the attention. Gerry continued to watch him. He had known Steve for ages on speaking terms, but he didn't really know the kid well – just the kid from the mail room. He must be shorter than Sue, he thought. A nice kid but such easy prey, so unsure of himself.

Steve said, "It's what she wanted and you know Sue."

He followed his own line of thought and lapsed into silence. Gerry let the silence grow. He wondered if Steve too could behave like the boy in the park. He was so ordinary but so had this Kevin been. He was just an office boy too, just someone like Steve. Somehow Gerry couldn't quite see Steve as a poofter basher. He smiled to himself. Who would see *him* as a killer either? Yet he was more proud of that than any other single action in his life. He was sure for once he had been right and that their action had been justified.

"You're not married, are you?" Steve knew he wasn't. "You wouldn't believe what it's like. All the organizing and that."

It seemed to Gerry that the kid couldn't unravel what he wanted to say.

"But it's worth it, isn't it?" Gerry helped him.

"I don't know." Steve scratched his head comically and gazed at the floor. "Everyone says it is. Everyone goes through it."

Then he looked at Gerry and added, "'Cept you."

"'Cept me," Gerry repeated.

And suddenly Sue was back with them and bristling to go. Her mother had packed them both sandwiches for lunch. They were saving now and buying lunch was a luxury. Gerry felt he ought to say something, so repeated to Sue, "I was just congratulating Steve."

He gave Steve a conspiratorial look. Steve smiled gratefully back. They were about to go when Steve turned back for a moment and said awkwardly, "Some of the guys are taking me for a drink tonight, do you want to come?"

Gerry paused. He never drank with the boys.

"It would be good if you could come," Steve urged.

"For once, why not," Gerry replied.

It was time the boys coped with him. He would phone Robert and let him know he was going to be late that evening. He would do it as soon as Sue and Steve cleared off.

He looked around. With all the work he wasn't sure he would get to lunch himself.

He worked right through lunchtime and got the quotas

under control. Having cleared the work from Sue's desk, they would both be ready for a clean break. Probably he had been a bit hard on her. Naturally she would be excited. He had just been edgy all day. Now at least they'd have nothing unpleasant to answer for at the next departmental meeting and could relax a little more.

At one-thirty, when he was just seeing his way clear to a break for coffee and the dizzy heights of the tea room, he was called into the office. The door was shut. It was obviously something major.

"Sit down Gerry," Wilson said, as he circled around to his own seat.

Once seated, he fingered at a piece of paper before him to give weight to what was to come. Then, coming to the point, he looked across and said, "Gerry, we've had a complaint from another member of staff."

"Oh?" said Gerry and waited.

Wilson seemed slightly unsure how to continue. It wasn't as he had rehearsed it. He tried again authoritatively, "Mrs O'Day says you upset her this morning. She says you called her a Nazi."

He looked at Gerry for a reply.

"Not exactly," said Gerry. "I just thought her attitude of shooting homosexuals on sight would find credence in the Third Reich. I told her so."

The older man looked flustered but went on, "Gerry, Mrs O'Day is a middle-aged woman. As such we should try not to upset her. We all know what she can be like, but just because you don't have the same kind of regard for women it does not give you the right to go upsetting her."

"Is that all?"

Connie being upset! Rather that than the police knocking on his door. It was so amazingly trivial. He had to stop himself laughing. Connie being upset! That was the crime he had to answer for. What about him being upset anyway? What about shooting down homosexuals in the park, Mr Wilson, what about that? Are you for it, against it or fence-sitting?

"No, that's not all. Gerry, you seem to have a problem

here. The other men, you don't get on with them. You don't try to be one of the team. Now it's for your own good I tell you this. Try adopting a more – a more masculine image.

"You're not, well, you're not what we would have called officer material in the forces. Not aggressive enough. I don't know what it is exactly, but the other men resent you for it. It will hold you back if you don't curtail it."

Christ, not aggressive enough now! If only they knew.

"Is there something wrong with my work?" he asked.

"Not exactly. It's attitude Gerry. Attitude and acceptability. Think about it. OK? It's for your own good I tell you.

"Now you have a think about it. Apologize to Mrs O'Day and we'll forget all about it. I'll tear up this complaint and we can call it closed. But Gerry, for your own good, try to be one of the boys."

They both sat in silence. The interview was over and he was expected to go back to work. He thanked his boss for the advice and left. Instead of going straight back to work, he stormed into the tea room. He didn't owe this place anything. It was the first time the straight man's creed had been put so solidly to him.

"Straighten up or you're out," he thought.

He laughed aloud at the hidden pun.

Neil was holding forth in the tea room, telling jokes. He had been inspired by the newspaper article to dig out all his old favourite poofter jokes for one more airing. His male audience guffawed in unison at all the old lines they'd heard before. Connie sat in the corner pretending it wasn't nice for a woman to understand such jokes.

As he made his coffee Gerry recited the jokes to himself in time to Neil's delivery. He knew them so well, in fact he could probably tell them better himself if he wanted to. Neil did a lousy job of aping a fag. When they got to the punchline, Gerry joined in aloud:

"And all he was left holding was a pair of fucking ears."

The joke fell flat as surprised eyes turned to look at

Gerry. He calmly poured the milk into his coffee, replaced it in the refrigerator neatly and sailed out the room saying, "Tell them about the two poofters who went straight-bashing, Neil."

Fuck the male world. Who wanted to be officer material in the forces anyway? If he had done, he would have joined the army.

So much for lunch. Sue was back when he got to his desk with his coffee. Steve had agreed to wearing the dinner suit but the next battle was teaching him the bridal waltz. He had confessed that he couldn't dance, another problem to beset the bride-to-be.

"And a guy called Robert phoned," she said, "but he didn't leave his number."

And that was all she knew of his private life. He was expected to share every twist and turn of her wedding plans, while his lover was to remain an unknown to her.

They got through the afternoon's work somehow. Wilson came through once and smiled weakly. Gerry just wanted to get away from the whole damned place. He felt tired and drained. He wished he hadn't promised to go for a drink and tried to think of a way to wangle out of it. He didn't want to offend Steve but he was hardly in the mood for a drink with the boys. Sitting there like a male spinster pretending not to understand the jokes and innuendoes. He had found in the past the most infuriating thing to do with sexist jokes was to pretend not to get them. The joker would in turn then have to explain the joke. This inevitably made it fall flat. If all else failed, he would reduce it with a statement like, "You mean she didn't want to fuck with him" or "Oh, the guy was sterile was he?"

The straight guys at work had given up on Gerry ages ago, assuming he had no sense of humour. In reality it was often aimed at them.

Steve made the unprecedented step of coming to get Gerry after work. He seemed scared Gerry would shoot through without the drink. He was right; it had been on the cards.

Things were a bit awkward at first but they went across

the the pub together and settled in the front bar. Steve looked pleased with himself but still had the same nervous air. He sat on his high seat looking at his beer and not knowing what to say. Gerry had a beer before him too. His was decorative; he hated beer.

"Well here's to the two of you," he said bravely.

He still didn't have the faintest idea why he was there but it had seemed important to Steve.

"Thanks," came the reply.

They sat in awkward silence. They hardly knew each other. It seemed doomed to be a failure.

"I never do this," said Gerry.

Why pretend he was unaware of his inadequacy?

"I'm not one of the boys, you know. I was told so in no uncertain terms today."

"What?"

Steve wasn't following.

"Never mind."

"No, what did you say?"

"Nothing. Where are the others?" Gerry asked.

Steve looked back at his beer. "There aren't any others. I only invited you."

He played with a water mark on the table. Searching for the words, he asked, "I want to tell you something, alright?"

"What?"

Gerry waited. There was a long pause while Steve assembled the words. At last he articulated simply, "I don't want to marry her."

"What?"

"I don't want to marry her. I thought you might understand. I just don't want to."

Again they sat in silence and looked at the table. Gerry studied the boy.

"You'd better tell her," he said softly.

"I can't."

He thought Steve was going to cry.

"How can I tell her? Everyone's expecting it now."

"The sooner you tell her the better."

"Yeah," he said and gulped at his beer.

"Why?" Gerry asked.

Steve said nothing for a while, then looked up: "What do you reckon?"

Their eyes met. The kid was really upset. Gerry was still unsure what he was trying to get at. He felt a coward. He reached for his drink, sipped it and tried to avoid pulling a face at the stale taste. Steve was still waiting for an answer. None came. He went on, "Reckon I must be a poofter."

And again it looked as if he was going to cry there in the front bar. Gerry said nothing. Then when Steve rubbed his hand across his face to wipe his eyes, Gerry said softly, "Only drunks cry in bars. Come on, let's get out of here."

He hoped the fresh air would do them good. Outside he was unsure what to do next.

"Let's walk. Then you can come back to my place for coffee," he suggested in desperation.

Steve looked bewildered. Gerry couldn't help it – he laughed. The kid thought he had been propositioned.

"No," Gerry said quickly, "there's someone I'd like you to meet. Let's walk up to get the car."

They were greeted as they walked through the door by the words: "What happened? I thought you were going out with the boys?"

"We decided to come here for coffee instead," Gerry retorted.

"Who's the we?" Robert asked eagerly, looking at the other arrival.

"Steve. He's the prospective bridegroom, only he isn't because the wedding's off."

It was abrupt enough even for Robert. Steve was wincing.

"What happened?"

"Nothing. He has had a change of mind, that's all."

"Sounds like a change for the better." Robert paused.

"Hi Steve, I'm Robert," he added.

Gerry was contorting his face into meaningful little signs. At first Robert refused to understand. Gerry persisted. Steve looked awkward. Robert knew perfectly well the uneasiness his presence was creating but hovered. Finally as if by inspiration he announced: "I'll make the coffee then." His smile swept the room and he sailed out.

Steve was furious.

"What are you doing. I didn't want you telling everyone. It was in confidence."

"It's only Robert."

"It's alright for you."

"Meaning what?"

The boy shrugged his shoulders helplessly.

"Look, we're only trying to help," Gerry continued.

Steve looked confused. Gerry said coaxingly, "You'll like Robert. Give it a chance. He has never met anyone from work before and he's a bit nervous. In fact he's scared stiff of you."

Robert drifted back tactfully to make amends for his last entrance. He certainly didn't seem scared stiff to Steve.

"Oh Gerry, did you see in the paper about that boy in the park? Awful. Make you stop before flouncing off on your own."

He explained to Steve, "Gerry always gets into such a tantrum about something or other and off he goes, out into the night."

It sat awkwardly. Robert was satisfied with the effect it had created. Gerry in turn was perfectly sure it was only by accident that Robert had hit on him flouncing off and that it was not connected in Robert's mind with the events in the park. He changed the subject.

"Steve just wanted some coffee, Robert, nothing more."

"Only if it's no trouble. I've got to be going soon."

"It's no trouble at all. Hold on." And Robert disappeared again.

"You don't have to go yet, you know."

"I'd better. I feel funny with him here. It's alright with you, but, I don't know . . ." he petered out.

"I wanted you to meet Robert just like Sue wanted me to meet you."

He realized the mistake after he had said it, so rushed on, "Robert's fine. He was married himself before we were lovers."

"Yeah."

Steve was all at sea. He hadn't heard men talk of each other as lovers before. It took him by surprise.

"Yeah, he went through with it and that was a real mistake. He'll tell you if you ask him."

"What was she like?" Steve asked.

"I don't know. I only met her once," Gerry replied. "It was at the hospital. She was allowed to see him as next of kin, I wasn't. Their divorce had already gone through."

"Any kids?" asked Steve.

Gerry shook his head. He wondered what had led him into this fairy godmother role with Steve. He fluctuated between enjoying and despising it. He felt he was expected to say to Steve, "Look, we're happy." It was like something in a Barbara Cartland novel.

Steve sat uncomfortably on the sofa. He gazed at the wall opposite. A drawing of a boy making love to a girl, with a skeleton arising, faced him. He looked away embarrassed. It was like something you shouldn't look at. Sue liked posters of still lifes, vegetables, that kind of thing. He hadn't known anyone with real art sort of pictures before.

Robert came in with the coffee. Steve saw the funny look he gave Gerry and the nod he received in reply. It was like some kind of code. He knew he was being classified and it made him uneasy. But the two poofs were right, he was one of them. That's what it meant, breaking off with Sue.

Robert prattled, "Do you suppose the papers are right claiming that boy was straight? I think it's just his mother. Such a pity. The boy is dead and his mother's main concern is that everyone knows he was straight. Poor little bastard."

"He could have been. You just don't know."

"Looks like a classic case of doing the beats to me. And they'll never catch the bastards who did it. The police don't try over-hard. Don't care. Another poof hits the dust, that's all it means to them. It's like sideshow alley to them, nothing more. Down goes another."

Gerry was looking a bit odd. Obviously he wanted Robert to be more discreet in front of Steve, but why should he? It was time people from Gerry's work met Robert. Besides he was going to impress upon the kid the danger of the beats. It would be a bonus to know what kind of thing could happen. So on he went: "It's hard for the police anyway. It's motiveless crimes like this that go unsolved."

Gerry butted in, "We don't know that it was motiveless. Anyway, Steve doesn't want to hear all this. He's got problems of his own tonight."

"Sorry I spoke," Robert mouthed pertly.

Steve sat feeling even more awkward. Even a lot of the language was unfamiliar to him. Nor did he want his troubles to become the centre of attention right now. He just wanted to drink his coffee and go. It wasn't that he didn't like Gerry. He felt wrong. He needed to be alone.

Robert had given him some pastry thing and a cake fork to eat it with. He couldn't use the fork and had shot crumbs all over himself when he tried. Gerry came silently to the rescue by using his fingers to eat his own. Robert noticed too, and felt guilty about it. Of course Steve wouldn't use a cake fork. On the other hand he would have to learn to overcome such things. Sooner or later he would need all the social skills he could muster amid elements of the gay community. Let him start to build his survival kit now, amongst friends.

"Will you talk to your parents first?" Gerry asked.

"Don't know. S'pose so. Mum will be pretty cut up. She was pretty keen on being a grandmother."

"Maybe you should just tell Sue."

"I don't know. I don't s'pose you could sort of . .?"

"No, I don't s'pose he could," cut in Robert. "You stay out of it Gerry. It's up to Steve."

"Yeah."

They sat on in silence. At length Steve said, "It's a nice

place."

The statement sat alone in the shared awkwardness.

"We've been here years," Gerry said absently.

"It's nice," Steve repeated.

Robert sensed he was the cause of the unease and considered finding another excuse to withdraw. He couldn't see why Gerry was getting involved. He was prepared to bet the boy would make the same mistake he had and go through with the wedding. Then it was kids like Steve who ended up having to do the beats to meet someone. He couldn't see what Gerry was getting uptight about. Steve was just the kind of kid who needed to be warned of the dangers it incurred, the kind of kid who ended up dead in the park with his mother pleading he was straight. At times Gerry was so prim about things like that. Warning Steve was surely best.

"You going to be alright?" asked Gerry.

"Yeah. I'd better be going now."

And he was on his feet to leave. Gerry guided him to the hall. Steve paused in the doorway.

"Is it OK if I talk to you again? After I've told her, I mean."

"Sure. Of course. And Steve."

"Yeah?"

"You'll be alright?"

"Yeah."

He went.

Robert heard the door close and was there in a moment.

"And what was all that about?"

Gerry explained as well as he could. Really there was little to say.

"That's what I thought," Robert rejoined.

Then returning to the kitchen, he proceeded to sing in bursts of falsetto, "I've got a crush on you."

"What's all this about?" Gerry asked at the door.

"Well, don't you think he has?"

"Steve? Don't be silly."

"Why not?" And Robert leered suggestively.

Sometimes Robert made Gerry feel such a heel. As long

as he never knew about Friday night.

Sue arrived late for work on Wednesday. Her eyes were red and swollen. Gerry didn't ask what was wrong.

Tuesday had been full of talk of wedding cars. She had greeted him on his arrival, not with an inquiry about the previous evening with Steve, but with the words, "Oh Gerry, good news about the cars. You won't believe it."

She had then gone on to explain she had found a hire firm that provided white Mercedes, complete with ribbons and a chauffeur, for only $150 each.

"They'll even match ribbons to the colour of the bridesmaids' dresses if need be."

The man had been so nice.

Three Mercedes with chauffeurs for $450, a real bargain. She would have to book early but it was such a find. Of course Steve would agree. He would get to ride in one after the ceremony after all. She'd always wanted to arrive at her own wedding in a white Mercedes.

Gerry had resisted saying anything. He considered putting the cat among the pigeons by suggesting, "Have you thought about a Rolls instead?"

It wouldn't have been kind. If only she had had the sense to ask about the previous evening. If only she hadn't been so blind to Steve's feelings. It was going to make it doubly hard for both of them. He felt guilty knowing what was going to descend upon her. He was also worried about Steve. The kid might not go through with it. He wasn't going to relish upsetting Sue. If he went through with the wedding it would only delay the heartache for Sue and increase it for himself, but people often goad themselves into easy solutions.

Gerry had been supportive to Steve on the Monday night and Steve in turn had been sure what had to be done. But while it was one thing to have the support of Gerry, who knew what would happen once the pressures of his family and peer group were reapplied? Gerry had wanted to show him that to be homosexual was not the end of the world or even a form of social leprosy. Had he succeeded?

Would it have any lasting affect? Conditioning was so strong.

The worst part of it was knowing Sue. For her sake too it should be called off. Unfortunately she would never see it that way. The dress, the cars, the day, were all more important than the groom. He was only subsequential to the total. That was probably how things had got this far. No wonder he was prepared to "wait". Neither were particularly interested in the relationship to follow.

And now it was Wednesday. Sue's eyes were burnt and sore. What a pair they made! Gerry still feared Robert would find out about Friday. Robert would not understand. Yesterday's papers had been quiet. It might still all pass by. A remark of Robert's stuck in Gerry's mind. Robert had said, "It's motiveless crimes like that that go unsolved." He had said it casually and perhaps he was right. If so, he need never know Gerry had gone out that Friday with the express purpose of being unfaithful to him. After ten years he had chosen that night. Now Gerry and five strangers shared in a conspiracy. After the blows of outrage, the silence of conspiracy. Yet he knew justice had been done. He believed there would be no further outcome. It had taken years of repression, and now there had been this backlash there would be no further reprisals. The act was complete in itself.

Sue sat down at her desk and looked straight ahead. She neither looked nor spoke to Gerry. He said good morning to her but kept on working. He knew that sooner or later he would have to look up. He put off the moment. What could he say? He wanted to look her in the eye and say, "It's not my responsibility."

If he had broken up with Robert and it was him sitting there with swollen red eyes, what solicitude would anyone offer? With Sue it would be as public as the wedding plans had been. He couldn't help feeling the difference. And it was that difference which made his loyalty be to Steve. Steve would need it around here. He was now on the outside too and they must stick together for support.

Silent support, like six men quietly leaving behind an assailant's corpse in a toilet block. The thought was ever with him.

Sue sat there and did nothing. Absolutely nothing. He felt the pressure to look up. After a while she said: "If Steve phones, I don't want to speak to him."

"Alright," he said and kept on working.

She turned her swollen eyes on him and watched him in silence. Her heart was broken, her plans dashed, and Gerry just worked on. For that moment she hated the middle-aged queer. Her eyes fixing him, she said, "Don't you even want to know?"

"No," he said and kept working.

She gazed around struggling for words. She couldn't comprehend it. Gerry worked quietly. He knew her anguish; he just didn't share it. No one had shared his. She must come through alone as he had. It was the law of survival that others had created for both of them. It wasn't of his doing.

"I don't, I don't . . . believe this. You don't even want to know."

"I do know," he said quietly and put down his pen. "I don't want to know but I do. I can't share your feelings, don't ask me to."

He put his head down again and continued to work.

She sat in a catatonic silence and he fought to isolate her from his own emotional state. One of them must work. He would carry her in that but in that alone.

After a while he heard her thrust her desk drawer open. He heard it bang shut and a magazine being thrown into the waste-paper bin. It thudded heavily against the tin. He didn't look up. He heard her chair squeak back and the rustle as she stood up to stalk off. He looked up only to see her retreating figure.

Steve had obviously told her that the wedding was off. If only she could have grasped the totality of the situation. They were now both saved from the charade of a marriage that could have satisfied neither. In time she would still have her home, husband and mortgage. The sacrifice had been from Steve. He could have had a life of furtive, casual sexual encounters, with her sitting at home waiting for him to return each night. His security could have been her uncertainty and doubt. Instead he had opted to be the outsider. She would get all the support she needed to recover from the broken engagement. No one would want to understand Steve's case.

So Gerry was not going to be one more voice to comfort her in support of her heterosexual aspirations. The girl had never had to question a single value before in her life. If lucky, she would be cushioned by friends through this experience and come out as unaware on the other side. How lucky she was. Born to be shielded by her own naivety. What would be Steve's buffer against the world? What had been Gerry's? Life in minority was hard enough, he was not going to waste his support on his unconscious oppressors. It was the values of the Sues of this society that keep him alien. What did it matter to him if there was one more broken engagement? He could never have one to break.

And Steve. He couldn't win now. Not until society changed. He had leapt out of the frying pan, yes – but into a fire in which he did not yet possess the skills to survive. Steve would now have to learn fast.

Gerry worked on. Half his brain worked on automatic, processing the chits before him.

It was nine-thirty and Sue still wasn't back at her desk. If Wilson came through he would be furious. Gerry reached over and pulled her pile of work towards him. He could get most of it processed quickly enough. He was a bit surprised to see quite how far back it went. She certainly had had her head in the clouds the day before. Skimming through it, it looked dangerously as if they would go over on the bookings again. There was nothing else for it but to get through it as quickly as possible.

Ten o'clock and still no sign of Sue. She couldn't still be in the toilets. Surreptitiously he left his work and started to make his way along to the toilets. He could at least get one of the girls to go in and see what had happened to her.

As he passed Wilson's office a voice called him in.

"Won't keep you a minute Gerry. I'm sure you have lots to keep you busy. Just thought I'd let you know I sent Sue to lie down for a while. You can keep up on your own, can't you?"

Of course he could, but he would rather do it off his own bat, than as an order. After all, he usually did. At least nothing more was said about upsetting Connie. He had stoically not said anything to her and was expecting to be pulled into line again over it. When Wilson had called out, he had expected the worst.

Still it was a bloody cheek the way they expected his support after Monday's reprimand. Wilson had always been a sucker for a pretty face, as long as she was kept junior to himself. He reminded Gerry of a teacher he had once had, who used to let the girls stand on a chair to clean the blackboard. It made their uniforms rise as they reached up to rub the board and the old boy had relished every rise and sway.

By morning tea time the whole office knew that the wedding was off. Both Pauline and Connie had been to tend to the needs of the shocked girl. Their diverse styles had ranged from, "He wasn't worth having anyway love", to Connie's more dour, "At least she had one. She doesn't want to end up an old maid."

"Old maid my arse," countered Pauline.

"Or worse," Connie added pointedly, her eyes on Pauline's rolls of flesh.

Gerry was hoping to be able to stay outside of the whole affair but when he went into the tea room there wasn't a space left for him to sit on his own. He had the choice of Neil or Pauline. Needless to say he chose Pauline. She was looking unusually solemn as she sat enveloping the chair beneath her humour-loving thighs.

Between their thick, black lines her eyes were alert to all the gossip that filled the air. Old Gerry would be the only one not to know. It wasn't that he didn't care, as Sue claimed. Gerry just wouldn't have registered. She sipped her tea and greeted him.

"You've heard about Sue, poor girl?"

"Yes, Steve told me on Monday evening."

The lines drawn around Pauline's eyes were stretched apart with surprise.

"You saw Steve on Monday evening? Christ, I'd shut up about that round here. They'll lynch you Gerry if they find out."

Pauline jumping in with her big mouth. She'd never acknowledged before that they all thought him queer. Now it had all popped out. He looked surprised.

"Oh, I'm sorry Gerry."

She shrugged her arms hopelessly and the flesh wobbled in echoes down to her reverberating chair.

To her surprise he smiled.

"I don't mind. I'm sure Connie would lead the lynching mob - but Steve? He's not my type."

"It's strange, isn't it? He always seems such a nice kid."

"Nice kids break engagements too."

"Yeah, I suppose so. Only I'm a romantic, you know Gerry. Always believing in Mr Right."

He egged her on, "So am I."

She couldn't help it. "Oh," she squealed and down thudded her palms onto those famous thighs.

People turned and looked. It wasn't suitable behaviour on this day of grief. Austerity was the order of the day. Connie looked over.

"Pauline! What if the girl was to hear you? After all she's going through. The man ought to be horsewhipped."

"Probably a lucky escape for both of them," Gerry crossed her. Pauline's eyes darted back and forth waiting for the retort. She secretly loved to see Connie crossed. The old wowser was bitchy enough about her when her back was turned.

Connie drew herself up with assumed dignity. "Well, that's what you would expect of you men. You all stick together."

Only Connie would see Gerry as one of the boys, for she was incapable of seeing beyond. It was a tribute to her lack of understanding.

Silence fell as Sue came into the room. She wove her way between the tables towards Gerry. She addressed him disinterestedly.

"Mr Wilson says you're to manage without me. He's going to run me home."

She turned around and withdrew as she had come. Silence reigned until her exit. The whole room heard her simple announcement. With the closing of the door the buzz of voices all started together.

"Doesn't she look terrible, poor girl?" Connie crooned.

"Can you manage on your own Gerry?" Pauline asked.

"Yes, but she's already sent us over on the 7.15."

"Shit. The shit will hit the fan if you don't sort that one out."

Pauline enjoyed the panic she had engendered.

"I think I've stopped them all in time," Gerry said wearily.

"Poor girl doesn't know what she's doing," Connie gloated. Her enjoyment came from the sense of tragedy. She always relished misfortune and was the first on the scene both for the commiserations and to start the grapevine of gossip.

Back at his desk Gerry knew he could manage. Solving past mistakes was the hardest part to tackle. If only she had concentrated a little more.

Half-way through the morning Wilson popped his head in to make sure all was running smoothly.

"I've taken Sue home, alright?"

And that was all he had to say. He just assumed he had Gerry's support. Gerry would manage.

Then the phone rang. It was Robert. He wasn't particularly interested in the news Gerry had about Sue. Instead he was full of the news about the boy found murdered in the park. The police had apparently released the fact that there had been a witness. It had just been on the radio. It was a friend of the dead boy who was with him at the time. They weren't saying any more but the appeal for others to come forward was again repeated. They can't have much, Gerry told himself, not if they are still asking for people to come forward. It was just a scare tactic.

What could a witness tell anyway? How could anyone else have known what happened there that night? Even for those inside the toilet block, it was too dark to see. Nor would they be able to identify each other. A passer-by would know nothing. They could only have seen a parked car, an anonymous figure in the darkness, but nothing more. And how many other shadowy figures had come and gone in the time immediately preceding and even after the event? Someone passing by minutes earlier or later would identify completely different cars or half-seen faces. The turnover there was fast. Gerry was safe. Nothing conclusive could be culled except from the six people present, and their common secret was safe.

To work, to work. Lunchtime was nearly on them and he was going to be kept pretty busy until Sue was back in action. He wondered how long it would take and what kind of advice and support she was receiving at home right now.

The phone rang again. It was Steve. Two personal calls in one morning. Gerry told him that Sue had gone home. He didn't say how badly she had taken it. It would be fatal to let the boy go back on it now. Now was the time to bolster him up most. If they were pressured back together now, they would stay that way.

Steve wanted to meet Gerry for lunch. Gerry thought it a bad idea. He remembered Pauline's reaction to his seeing Steve on the Monday evening. It would obviously make it worse for the kid if they were seen together at lunchtime today. Even if eventually Steve was going to have to face the lash of rumours that surrounded Gerry's working life, today was not the day to start. It could cause just the sort of panic to send Steve back to Sue and the bridal arrangements. If Steve was to come out even that far at work, it must be in the climate of his choosing.

When he turned down the lunchtime meeting, Gerry thought Steve sounded disappointed. He so obviously needed support. Gerry decided to explain it with a half-truth by saying how frantic it was without Sue, and that lunch, in any shape or form, might be out of the question. He then tried cushioning the refusal by saying, "Robert phoned before to ask after you."

"Yeah?" But it didn't seem to have the desired effect.

Steve started on dangerous ground: "You know I do still care about Sue a lot."

"Of course you do," Gerry countered. "And that's why you had to call it off and why you now have to keep it that way. It's for her sake too."

"Yeah, I know. Only . . . was she very upset?"

Gerry paused and then decided on the truth. "Yes. But she'll get over it."

"Yeah. I suppose."

Gerry caught sight of Wilson's passing back. He continued to talk anyway. The kid was more important. If it had been Sue talking to Steve it would be condoned by all, so what the difference?

"How are things at home?" he asked.

"Pretty bad. Mum isn't speaking to me this morning."

"She'll get over it too, you wait and see."

"I don't know. She was pretty mad at me last night."

Gerry could just imagine. He suspected she wouldn't get over it either. This could well be the beginning of Steve's alienation from them. His mother wouldn't get over it but with any luck Steve would, in time.

"My brother reckons the old man is going to throw me out. Hasn't said anything to me though."

"If he hasn't, he probably won't. You might find he's quite supportive if you give him a chance."

"He's not the kind of bloke you can talk to."

"Don't then, leave him be."

"Yeah, I reckon you're right."

Gerry really should get back to work now. He tried easing the call to an end without offending Steve. Just when he was about to hang up Steve asked, "Can I come over and see you tonight? If it gets too rough, I mean."

Gerry had to agree. Steve had to know that he had some support. It was probably right it should come from Robert and himself. At least Steve must have overcome his fear of Robert if he wanted to come back. That was a start. No one from work need know he was coming over.

Gerry took a short lunch-break in the tea room rather than going out to risk running into Steve. It was peculiarly quiet. Only Connie sat there doing her lottery numbers. Apart from her, the tea room was empty. They ignored each other as long as possible. Gerry scouted around for an afternoon paper but with no luck. He wondered if the papers would have a more detailed release than the radio had. Actually Robert seemed to care more than he did. He hoped Robert knew and suspected nothing.

When she had finished filling in her coupons, Connie rose and addressed the room in general, "I suppose someone ought to phone the poor girl."

He thought it very unwise. Since there was no one else present, he tok it on himself to reply.

"You do that," he said.

For once she seemed satisfied.

"It happened to my eldest," she said as she rinsed out her tea cup. "Engagements always seem to be on and off at least once."

"And she's alright, isn't she Connie? She got over it?" he asked.

"Oh yes, they got over it and got married." Then she continued more to herself, "Course they aren't happy now. He just didn't change after they were married. Not the way she was hoping he would."

"Did she?"

"Did she what?"

"Did she change Connie, after they were married?"

"Jossie? No. Why should she? She wouldn't change, she's like her mother."

Gerry sat on in the tea room alone. He would have liked to phone Robert to find out about the news report but decided it would be unwise to show so much interest. Wisest to let it rest.

After about twenty minutes he returned to his desk. The

afternoon flow was already starting to come through and it was a matter of pride that he was going to keep up alone. He couldn't call it loyalty for he felt he owed the place little enough. No one acknowledged the lost lunch-breaks, they only noticed when things went wrong.

He was back at his desk working steadily as the rest of the building crawled back into motion after their break. Everything seemed to be going well.

It was about two-thirty when Wilson came storming through. Pauline had brought the morning's figures from the counter and as she had predicted, "The shit had hit the fan."

"Gerry," he barked, "the 7.15 for the twelfth has gone over and I'm holding you responsible. The numbers have come from your section and your section alone. If they had been processed immediately instead of sitting around . . ."

"I'm short-staffed," Gerry answered back.

"What?"

"I'm short-staffed. I'm here alone."

"Sue's only been away half a day."

"Then it's probably her booking."

He felt disloyal saying it but why should he take the rap?

"I don't care whose booking it is, you're responsible for this section and it's for you to sort it out."

"I'll fix it up if you give me the details."

"Wasting time on the phone while work sits around, then this happens."

Gerry ignored the comment. He could pretend it was being applied to Sue not himself. He took the details and studied them slowly. More embarrassing calls to make. He was good at that. Sue's writing sure enough.

"And another thing,"

"Yes?"

"Have you spoken to Mrs O'Day yet?"

Gerry shook his head.

"Well I would if I were you."

And he returned as he had come.

Gerry had seen the scene a hundred times before. He

would love to just quit the job but he couldn't afford to. After all, it helped support his life at home with Robert and that was what mattered, wasn't it? He didn't believe anyone found job satisfaction anymore, just sustenance for the hours they lived away from the place.

He just wanted to clear up the mess, finish up and go home. Surely he and Robert could help sort out something for Steve?

The boy in the park was dead. There wouldn't be a witness. If he held on, things would return to normal.

Three

It was odds on that he would get a hard-on with the kids jumping on him like that. One of the problems of being popular with the boys. At times like these he felt so randy he wanted to fuck the lot of them. If only they knew. Or their parents. Shit, that would do it! But Phys. Ed. teachers don't fuck boys. The Art Department was always far more suspect for that, or the English mob. Trouble was all the fags there were straight – as far as he could tell anyway.

This was the last lot of the day. It had developed into a right free for all. His prick was going to burst out of his jocks if they didn't lay off. Great it would look, walking across the yard in his tracksuit with a hard-on. Those things didn't hide anything and Robbo knew he was well hung and had plenty to hide.

He blew his whistle and they all reluctantly clambered off him. His watch showed it was only five minutes to go. He could send them off for showers now. He gave the order from a sitting position, his knees bent up to protect his throbbing bulge from sight. Christ, after all these years it still gave him a hard-on.

He couldn't trust himself to see them into the showers. All those fourteen-year-old arses displayed outwards as they protectively hid their pricks towards the wall. Only once had he showered with them. His great penis had caused enough excitement that day as it proudly trailed its way to the shower. And it hadn't even been erect. God knows how he had kept it down. He wasn't going to risk it again. Graffiti had shown him with a twenty-four inch dick for all the rest of the year. It still popped up that way occasionally even today. It was kind of flattering. No one could say the kids hadn't been interested. That too excited him in a way. The possibility was there with lots of them. The parents made it an impossibility, but some of them were as randy as he was and knew what it was all about. He let the horseplay go in the changing-rooms, ignoring the supposed protests of the participants. He'd been through it all himself. Scared it wasn't masculine to fancy other boys.

He ran his hand through his short, cropped hair. He had been sweating with the excitement. It was over now and he could get up and follow the boys back towards the school buildings. He was dying for a cigarette. He walked over the butts that littered the ground around the gardener's shed. All the staff knew the kids smoked there, it just wasn't worth the hassle of trying to stamp it out. The boys didn't even have the sense to cover their own tracks. They thought they were so grown-up, but they were still just kids.

He had a golden rule that kept them out of bounds. After his final year at teacher's college, he had vowed to himself that he would never fuck with any of them, students or ex-students. To be accurate, at the time he had vowed not to fuck with anyone. That hadn't lasted out the summer vacation. Now it was just the kids that were taboo. It had been so for eight years now.

The bell went. His class was emerging from the shower block fast enough. He wouldn't have to chase them out like he did in the middle of the day. The last classes always changed fast. It meant he could get away on time too.

No reason to go back into the staffroom and all the bitching talk he would encounter there. Teachers only ever talked shop. He had nothing to do with them inside working hours or out. He just threw his dirty gear into his locker each week until the vice-principal complained about the smell in the staffroom. He got off on it himself. It was sweaty, moist and stale – just like semen. No wonder those prudes complained about it. It was pretty uncompromisingly male.

He cultivated his supermale ego before them. The cropped hair, bristling moustache and strong chest held no other implications for them. They thought him too busy with his mates to get married. So he was – too busy screwing them. He should come out with them at work but it suited him this way. No one would go delving into his past for dirt to chuck around, so he let things ride and fostered their ignorance. Jesus, he could upset the vice-principal enough just by sweating. She found both the sight and odour offensive. To really rile her he had been known to spit in the yard, not to mention going into the staffroom in his bathers before he took the school swimming. Boy, he loved those swimming lessons! Wet speedos and white bums. But he never got into the water with them, never touched anyone. Let them do the jumping, the splashing, the touching, the feeling. He guessed he was just a perv with fantasies.

He swaggered out of the gate with the first of the kids. The principal would be watching but what the fuck – that man was a pushover. Besides, Robbo was good with the kids. No discipline problems, few truants, no complaints from parents and that was what the Department liked, that was what the principal liked. He gave them the commodity they sought and made it clear that they got no extras. It worked well for everyone. In eight years not a single complaint about him. Couldn't beat that as a record. Jesus, some of the teachers had about one parent up there a week – matched the number of kids they molested. Some of the chicks working there were hopeless. Monica laid into the kids, open sandals and all. She used to say get them early in the day, then the marks wore off before they got home.

He slammed his old VW into action. Its revs screamed louder than the kids spilling out through the gates. When he started up, they got out of the way. They showed him a degree of reverence or fear – he wasn't sure which.

At home he just threw off his clothes and flopped out on the bed. The room was a mess; his body still moist and clammy.

He gazed up at the ceiling and blew smoke-rings towards it meditatively. It relaxed him. Jesus, the room was in a mess. One day he would have to open a window or something and let some air in – it was putrid. His clothes sat around so long between washes, they needed burning. Burn baby. The thought made him smile. Absent-mindedly he started to play with himself. Not that he wanted to get off, he was feeling good and it relaxed him further. It blocked out thoughts. Let his tool be the only active part of his body. He finished his smoke and stubbed out the butt on a saucer next to the bed.

He laughed to himself. He remembered the judge looking so offended. And he fell asleep.

His body was well trained. He woke at six-thirty. It only took a few seconds to come round. Time to get up and go up to the market at the local shopping centre. It was late night shopping so he still had an hour and a half. He would make it easily. He poured himself an orange juice from the refrigerator and climbed into some old jeans he had left lying on the floor. They were a pretty tight fit and he wasn't wearing any jocks, so he had to be careful with the zipper. He shoved his prick down the left leg to show an obvious bulge. The roughness of the material excited him slightly, making the bulge grow more prominent. He was raring to go tonight. He looked in the mirror. You couldn't miss a prick like that. He threw on a sweater, sculled the juice and was set to go.

The shopping centre was a pool of stark neon light and bustling people. Fuck, he hated crowds. He swaggered through them and they parted before him. He went past the supermarket and the small-goods section to the fruit and veg market. He tried to be careful about what he ate, plenty of fresh fruit and veg. His body was the food he put into it and he tried to keep it in top form. He knew he could make people stop and look and he swaggered more to prove it. The confinement of his cock in the tight jeans was keeping it semi-erect.

But it was time to apply his mind to what he needed for

the weekend. He strolled along the crowded aisle surveying the goods laid out there. He always selected carefully before he bought. First time round was just a reconnaissance; the second time round he bought. It wasn't worth saving a few cents to lose the quality. From each stall he bought only what was best.

While he was looking at some oranges, he saw a guy with longish hair and a neat little arse saunter past. He was carrying a cardboard box half-full of vegetables on his hip. It accentuated the slight sway of the slim hips as he walked. Robbo watched his arse proceeding up the aisle between the two rows of stalls.

"I'll have him," he decided then and there.

His crotch was thinking not his mind, but then his crotch did a better job than his brain. True it would be good if both worked together, his crotch to lead him into trouble and his brain to get him out of it, but then that wouldn't be Robbo. He had paid heavily for such impetuous acts in the past and would again no doubt. He was careful at school – but here? Hell, why not? If he wanted to screw the guy, then he wouldn't let up till he had.

Firstly he had to get the guy's attention. The guy was as yet unaware of Robbo's existence. He followed him round the stalls to check him out properly. Yes sir, he was what he wanted. So Robbo cut through to the next aisle. This way he would be coming towards the guy as he came up the next row of stalls. He stationed himself conspicuously halfway along and waited. He could see the guy coming towards him unawares. For a second the crowd parted and Robbo caught his eye. It had been brief but something had registered.

Slowly the guy moved closer. He was aware of the watching eyes now, Robbo could tell by the way he avoided looking up. He too was playing the game.

Then suddenly he was coming straight towards Robbo, his eyes resting inquiringly on him. Robbo casually slid his hand up his thigh to his crotch, and gazing directly at the guy, lightly rubbed his prick to emphasize its presence.

The guy smiled but looked away. He knew what was going on; it was just unclear as yet if he was going to take it up.

No one turned Robbo down. The guy wasn't getting away with that. The neat little arse was calling him on. If he brazened it through, Robbo thought he could pull this one off.

He followed the arse to the small-goods stall, where the guy waited to be served. He looked round once and knew Robbo was still there. Robbo waited well back, leaning against a pillar with his hands through the belt loops on his jeans. His strong, heavy hands rested in two crescents around his zipper. It was his favourite open position. His intention was apparent but who could accuse him of stating it? The women going past were probably admiring his dick too. People did. He like to show it off.

With his purchases finished, the guy put his box on the ground and knelt down to pack in the new items. He looked up. He could see Robbo's prick summoning him. He looked and considered, then went back to rearranging his box. Unsure if the chance would get away if he left it any longer, Robbo moved in. He stood before the kneeling figure with his crotch pushed forward to the guy's face.

The guy looked up. Robbo smiled down at him.

"Hi," he said.

"Good day."

The number looked embarrassed but rose to a standing position. He smiled nervously.

"Haven't seen you around here before," Robbo stated.

The guy shrugged. Robbo looked at his crotch. The guy knew that he was being assessed. Robbo let his own crotch swell slightly for its newly captured audience. The guy's eyes flashed down to the movement then back up to Robbo's face.

"You live round here?" Robbo asked.

"Yeah – with friends."

The guy was starting to relax. Robbo was now sure he was going to get there.

"How much time you got?"

The quarry paused.

"For what?"

"Thought we might have time for sex, man," Robbo replied.

The guy laughed.

"Fine," he said. "Where?"

Robbo whacked the arse lightly on the left cheek and grinned.

"Follow me," he said.

He turned and led the way through to the car park, then on to the metal door next to the lift shaft. It was a public area but badly lighted. The guy carried his box in front of him. Robbo held open the emergency exit door for him, then let it slam shut. It echoed up and down the shaft like a cell door banging shut at night. Before proceeding he reached under the box and gave the guy's prick a good feel. It was coming up already.

They went up the metal staircase, Robbo leading the way almost disinterestedly. Only at the top floor did he look back. The guy was just behind him. He pushed the door open, then it too slammed behind them. The second door to the cell block. The guy looked around; they were on the roof of the car park, open to the sky. It was dark already; stars gleamed very far above. The air was still; there were no cars in sight. Robbo led his quarry to the dark gloom behind the top of the stairwell and lift shaft. It would be fairly private there.

He took the guy's box from him and pushed him up against the wall. Holding the guy there with one arm, he squeezed his crotch hard with the other hand. It wasn't clear if he was going to rough the guy up or have it off. Robbo twisted his hand hard on the penis it held. The guy let out a gasp. Robbo pressed in hard on him pushing him to the wall and attacking the gasping mouth in a rough, forceful series of kisses. This was how he liked it. The guy was scared. He squealed and struggled. Robbo pinned him there, his mouth clammed over the other's. With his free hand he undid the belt and forced the guy's jeans half down about his knees. He yanked hard on the erect cock. Then he slipped his own erection out and started to pound it into the guy before him. His hand went up inside the shirt and pinched and twisted the nipples there. The more his partner squirmed, the more he forced himself onto him.

He tore at the nipples and pounded his throbbing dick into the guy's stomach. His mouth smothered the gasping mouth beneath, chewing at the ears, chin and neck, leaving bite marks to bruise and scar. His partner must have been having one hell of a time: he was squealing with delight.

"Turn around," Robbo ordered into the ear he was smothering.

The guy was shaking his head frantically.

"No," he gasped, "I don't fuck."

"Don't fuck – Jesus."

Without further words, Robbo took the guy's head between his hands. He held it firm enough to avoid escape and guided it down to his erection. "Suck," he ordered.

He thrust his penis into the mouth before him. He battered it in and out as hard as he could, holding the guy's head so that he couldn't resist. He heard the guy spluttering, "Shit, man." But he kept on pumping; the throat would have to take it. He thrust away cruelly until finally he felt himself on the verge of coming. Then he held the head still for a moment and drew back. Then it was on again. He bore it quickly in and out until he felt himself shoot into the unwilling throat. The guy was choking as he withdrew.

He shook the last of the semen from his tool and forced it back into his pants. As he walked away the other guy was still on the ground spluttering. Robbo had his marketing to do. The guy could find his own way down.

Back in the well-lit shopping area Robbo discovered he had a damp stain on his fly. He rubbed it and went to buy his provisions.

He laughed as he thought of the judge's face. Loitering, the charge had been. Convicted of the intent. No action was necessary in those days. He had been charged with intending only. Shit, if every bastard was convicted on his thoughts alone, at nineteen they would all be on the inside. Gays and prostitutes were the last to be labelled with it. In that final year at college both could still be charged for contemplating activity. Loitering and soliciting they called it.

He sniggered at the thought. If prostitution was something prostitutes did, surely soliciting was how solicitors made their living.

Back home it was time he got something to eat and finally have a shower to get rid of the smell of the day's sweat. He tackled the food problem first. He left out one of the apples he'd just bought and ate his way through it as he packed the rest of his purchases away.

To look after his body he had to eat properly so he cooked himself a T-bone and threw together some salad as it was grilling. At times he could be picky about food. No fast-food junk found its way into his diet. His body was about all he valued and he wanted to keep it that way.

He shoved vitamin pills down in the morning and made sure he got a decent workout at school. Shit, so many teachers taught Phys. Ed. sitting on their arse and issuing instructions. It was no joke. How could they expect to keep fit and get the kids going that way? Besides, he enjoyed the physical exertion of doing everything along with them. Unless he raised a sweat, he couldn't expect them to. It gave him a kind of a high to feel them all there pushing themselves along with him. The principal would say he was good at his job, but really he just got off on it.

He cleared a space on the table and ate his steak and salad. The shit food they sold at work appalled him. Often he'd had a go at both the kids and the women in the canteen about it. The silly bitches in the shop had lost track of their purpose and just looked to profits like a commercial concern. Instead of changing the kids' eating habits, they pandered to them. Coke and potato chips for lunch was fine by them. The result was that the kids were all constipated and farted through any unexpected physical exertion. Gymnastics was fatal. But shit, school was out, and he could forget it for another twelve hours.

He finished eating and left his plate where it was, wandering off to the bedroom. He stepped out of his clothes and left them there on the floor. That was where he had found them an hour and a half earlier. At least they got an airing in between. He had the shower hot, spending as long under it as he could until the water started to run cold. Every part of him had been soaped, soaked and was clean and ready for the night. He dried himself thoroughly, making sure he dried between his toes, up around his arse, every cranny clean and dry. Looking in the mirror, he really needed a shave. He ran his hand over the stubble thoughtfully and decided to leave it. It suited him not to look groomed. Besides it felt great as it pricked into the flesh of his hand. Some kind of thrill there for whoever he met tonight.

Back in the bedroom, he decided he'd take the bike again tonight. The clapped out old VW didn't command the right image. Deciding against any underwear, he pulled on a clean pair of jeans and a check shirt. Boots and a leather jacket, and he was just about set to go. He looked in the mirror and rearranged his cock. The rest was satisfactory. He could make a start for the night.

He kick-started the bike into action and cruised to the end of the block. Nine o'clock. A bit early to make a start. He'd go for a ride first.

Heading in the right direction, he cruised every park and every bog on the way. Twice he did the lap around the football ground. Both bogs at either end were quiet. The light was still working in each. No cars in sight. Not a single jogger still about. It was going to be a lousy evening. He didn't even bother to stop the bike and take a closer look. Cars were the best indication and without one parked outside, hardly anyone was going to bother to stop. It just took one to park and within minutes others would materialise. No one came to the oval on foot. It was too far except for runners. Nine-fifteen, a bit late for runners.

He cruised on down to the park at the city's edge. Pretty dark. No light inside and two cars left in the shadows. One had a kid's sticker on the window. Sloppy bastard, he thought, but he decided to give it a try anyway.

He crunched through the door in his heavy boots, his helmet under his arm. Two frightened figures sprang apart. One had been giving the other a head job while he sat on the dunnie and wanked himself off. Robbo wasn't interested. It crossed his mind to ask which one had the kids. It might fuck things up so he let it be. He made towards the urinal while the two figures scrabbled to get respectable in the cubicle. To save them coming out he hissed, "It's cool, mate, keep going."

There was silence, then the squelching sound of an amateurish blow job being continued. He turned and left.

Just one bog left to cruise, then the pub. It was one of the last of the cast-iron pissoirs left in the city. A monument to the Victorian beats, still functioning on both levels. Leaving his bike, he went inside. There were two separate urinals. A figure stood at one. He took up the other. The guy stretched over to see his dick. He jerked it then looked at his neighbour. It was a kid of about seventeen. Nervous, straight out of school, with nowhere better to go. The kid took the look as interest and reached over to grab Robbo's dick. Robbo drew back. He'd promised, no kids. Besides, he remembered being seventeen and doing the beats with nowhere to go and no idea what to do. His sex life had consisted of coquettishly wanking at his dick until someone showed interest, then rushing off home alone. Something in the kid made it all come back to him.

"No thanks, kid," he said, stuffing his dick away.

The kid looked scared and disappointed but Robbo knew he wouldn't give up for the night. He'd stay on there hoping until the police or trouble ferreted him out.

"Try the sauna, kid."

The boy looked surprised.

"Have you got any money?"

The boy looked bewildered.

"Here's ten bucks, go to the sauna. Across the way from the museum station."

He thrust the money at the kid. Something dawned.

"You mean it's dangerous here?"

"Too right. Now get to it."

Still the kid stood there.

"You know where the sauna is?"

The kid nodded.

"I'm telling you then, piss off."

And he left.

As he started his bike the kid emerged from the pissoir. He looked over to Robbo. Robbo waved his arm in the direction of the sauna. The kid nodded and waved back. Robbo didn't wait to see if he had understood the direction. He found he was sweating. It was the thought of the first guy he had picked up in a bog. The memory of it always brought out a sweat.

When he finally got to the pub, he had to push his way through the crowds to get a beer. Once served, he turned round, leaning with his back to the bar to survey the throng and make his choice. The place was really hopping for a Thursday night. The crowd was a fairly mixed lot. A lot of the faces he knew, but they weren't there to socialize. He exchanged a few nods of acknowledgement, nothing more. He decided to lean back and let himself be hustled, let someone else do the work after his first exploit for the night. He was displayed well enough. He made himself available and was sure enough of himself to just let it happen.

Sipping his beer, his eyes casually spanned the room. The space-invader machines were doing great business. High scoring here in all regards. The younger group seemed to congregate there. Outside, through to the beer garden, looked quieter. It was always an older crowd sitting out there. Most of them arrived in pairs and weren't part of the market; just there to meet and bitch with old friends.

Robbo lounged on up against the bar. After a while he

became aware that a face through the crowd was trying to catch his eye. He leant back on the bar and sipped his beer. He gave nothing away. His drink was nearly finished. A figure pushed through the crowds and up to him, ostensively to get a drink.

"Hi," the guy said as he pushed through to the bar.

Robbo nodded.

"It sure is crowded here tonight."

There was a slight accent that Robbo couldn't place. "Always jumping on a Thursday night," he replied.

The guy waited there in silence. He was facing the bar but in no hurry to be served.

"Can I get you a drink?" he asked.

Robbo had made sure his glass was empty.

"Beer," Robbo replied and waited.

The guy turned his back and attracted the barman's attention. He had a good arse, Robbo noted. He bought two beers, handing one to Robbo.

"My name's Angel," he smiled.

"Angel! What kind of a name's that?" Robbo asked.

"Just my name, I guess." He paused.

"Where you from?" Robbo asked.

"I live here two years, before that, New York City."

"Yeah, but you got an accent."

"Well, I'm from Puerto Rico before that."

"Puerto Rico, eh!"

"Yes, Puerto Rico." He smiled and looked as if something important had been established.

"And you?" he asked.

"Me? Born here."

Robbo sipped his beer and gazed absently away. He'd have this one anyway, so may as well make the guy work at it. He didn't look bad. Pretty dark. Robbo thought he might have an uncircumcised cock. He could see it was a fair size.

"I live here two years with a lover but it didn't work out," Angel continued.

"Tough."

Robbo wasn't at all interested.

"I met him in New York and came here to him but no good. He play around, you know."

Robbo looked at the anxious face. He couldn't give a shit.

"What are you doing here tonight then, mate?"

"It's all over now, I move out."

"Will you go back to New York?" Robbo thought he'd better play him along a bit.

Angel paused, unsure how to answer.

"What's it like there anyhow?" Robbo asked.

"New York? Well, you know anything about horses? New York City is like a bronco horse. Once it's been messed up, you know, wrongly broken, then it's out of control for all time. That's New York City."

"Shit, I've never heard a city compared to a horse before. You're crazy, man."

"Yes I'm crazy." And Angel smiled happily.

Robbo leant back on the bar, arching his back and thrusting his crotch foward. Angel's eyes watched eagerly.

"And I'm one horny guy," Robbo replied.

"I like to fuck," Angel stated.

"That's great by me. Give me time to finish my drink."

"I can fuck three, four times a day," Angel went on, "but with my lover it was no good. He was tired all the time, from screwing around. Once a month if I'm lucky, that all we had sex."

I'll have to fuck him soon, Robbo thought, it's the only way of shutting him up.

"I left my country because it very hard there to be gay. My family would feel shame. My mother, she very old now, but she very well-known woman. She couldn't face the shame."

"Is that right?" Robbo said absently.

"Yes. The police they phoned her once when they saw me in a gay bar. She very angry so I said I just walked in and out again. I was so shocked."

"Come on. She didn't believe you?"

"She believe me. I was married with two kids then."

He stopped and grinned, "Then I find I like men more."

"So goodbye Argentina."

"Not Argentina, Puerto Rico."

"Sorry mate."

Angel looked around and finally sipped his drink. Then he came back with the words, "I don't know no one here, do you?"

"Heaps," Robbo replied. "You found your way here alright."

"I'm very shy person really." And again he smiled.

If only the guy would talk less and smile more Robbo could put up with it a bit longer. His body was pretty good and the dark skin could be a real turn-on. He hadn't known any South Americans before. It hadn't occurred to him that there were many gays there.

"Police hassle you much at home?"

"At home?"

"In Puerto Rico."

"No. No, it my family. That's why I go to New York but they treat you like shit there. Just a piece of meat, that's all."

"You got to be rich to live in New York?"

"Rich and white," he said bitterly.

"You got a black dick?" Robbo asked.

Angel laughed. "You only interested in my dick?"

"Yeah, that's right." And Robbo grinned back.

"Where can we go?" Angel asked.

"I'll borrow the key to the storeroom. One of the barmen is a mate of mine. Hold on, I'll be back."

Robbo contemplated abandoning the guy but if they fucked at least it would shut him up. Besides he wanted to see the black dick. There weren't many of them around.

He got the key from Rick and came back through the crowds to where he had left Angel at the bar.

"It's alright," he said, showing the key. "Rick might come in if he can get away."

"Rick?"

"Yes. He likes to watch."

The key to the storeroom was just about anyone's on that one condition. Angel nodded understanding and the two headed off towards the back room. As they pushed through the crowd, disinterested heads turned knowingly. Nearly everyone ended up either in the toilets or the back room during the course of the evening.

Robbo led the way into the room and closed the door. He took off his jacket and rested it on a pile of cartons near the door. Angel turned around and smiled at him. Robbo moved in to be greeted by Angel's eager mouth in a prolonged full kiss. Angel's mouth twisted, turned and devoured as he forced his tongue into Robbo's throat. The kiss was returned in kind, rough and pressing.

Angel's hands worked at Robbo's shirt, undoing the buttons and getting inside. Jesus, this guy knew how to get you going. Robbo let Angel work on his nipples as he peeled off the shirt with his free hand and started to unbuckle his jeans. As soon as his shirt was off, Angel went down sucking and biting at Robbo's nipples.

Shit, this guy was hot. He unzipped Robbo's jeans and thrust his hand in to yank out the cock, pulling on it hard as he bit and chewed at Robbo's chest. Robbo arched back and let it happen, then slid his hand down to unleash Angel's zip. Angel stopped to give him a hand, stripping down his pants to reveal his erection.

Jesus, his cock was dark and huge. Robbo grabbed at it and started tugging as Angel went down on him and sucked his cock hard, working steadily from head to base in long thrusts. His hands gripped Robbo's buttocks exploring for his arsehole. One finger dug in sharp and probing. Robbo gasped out and pulled harder on the large black cock. He forced Angel off and bent-over to suck his cock in turn. It tasted good in his mouth. Angel lent over the crouching back and massaged the cheeks.

"You've got a great arse man, let me have it."

He turned Robbo round and spat on his hand to massage the end of his cock. Robbo bent forward and Angel was straight in. Robbo groaned. The pain felt like fire inside him. Holding Robbo in a bent-over position, Angel held the inside of his thighs and jabbed in and out of his anus. Then he penetrated deep and started to fuck steadily in long slow gyrations.

Robbo hadn't felt it like this for years. Angel pinned him round the middle with one hand and grabbed his cock with the other. He masturbated Robbo in time with his own fucking motion and it felt great. Jesus, you never could tell what you were getting. The guy had said he liked to fuck but Robbo had assumed he would do the fucking. Both his prick and his arse felt like they would burst.

"Hold on man," Angel said, "I'm not ready yet." He drew back and again took hold of Robbo's hips. He twisted and turned his erection in and out the length of Robbo's anal passage. It felt great. He gyrated with the power.

Robbo hadn't been fucked like this for God knows how long. He hoped Rick wouldn't be in to see it. Robbo didn't like it to get around that he enjoyed taking it too.

"Finish off man, I'm bursting," he cried.

Angel stabbed back and forth deep into him and fucked quick and sharp to finish off. He masturbated Robbo with one hand, gripped at his balls with the other. Robbo shot first. Angel was seconds later. He withdrew quickly and turned Robbo around, kissing him ferociously on the mouth. Then they stepped apart.

"You're one hell of a fuck," Robbo said. He couldn't help himself.

"Beautiful arse," Angel retorted.

Robbo slipped his shirt on and pulled up his jeans. He got his prick back inside but the zipper wouldn't close. Angel laughed. He was dressed ready to go.

"You want another drink?" he asked.

"I want a cigarette and to get my prick down enough to get my fly up first," Robbo replied.

He pulled his stomach in and the zip came up. Grabbing his jacket, they unlocked the door and returned to the other room.

Back at the bar Angel looked at Robbo mournfully and said, "My mother is a very old woman now but I can't go back and see her. The family are so shamed. It's not the same as here. When I last saw her she was fifty but still very beautiful; now she's old. I like to go back and see her but I come here instead. I come here to be with my lover and all he do is play around. What you think?"

Robbo looked back bewildered. "About what?"

"You think I should sit home while my lover plays round?"

Robbo thought of the backroom.

"Shit no," he said, "I reckon you should use what you got. You use it pretty well."

"Thank you," Angel said and looked pleased. "Back home you know . . ."

Robbo stubbed out his smoke and cut him off. "Look I've got to be going now. Hope I see you again soon."

Angel looked surprised as Robbo started to push away through the bar. Then he turned and said, "Angel, you're a terrific fuck", and was gone.

Robbo stood outside to get some air. His arse was sore. It was still retracting from Angel's presence. His head felt light. He'd had only two drinks, he didn't want any more. The street was dark. He could hear noises coming from the bushes along the footpath. It was an old, narrow surburban street. You half expected old ladies to watch from behind lace curtains. Some people would fuck anywhere. The police could get them for that. He always chose his places more carefully. Well, he did now anyway. The grunts from the undergrowth continued.

He took in a long breath of air. He would go for a spin and get a proper breeze. After that – well, he could manage at least one or two more tricks for the night.

He rode down across the bridge and along the river. It was still, quiet and dirty. The Yarra had been a source of jokes for years. Sometimes couples copulated on its banks. Not tonight. The Yarra was too dead even for that these days. He took the road up towards the War Memorial and around the Domain. It was quiet there too. A lone soldier could usually be seen guarding the eternal flame. He wondered what they did if it went out.

Sometimes you could pick up the soldier there for a quick fuck in the nearby toilets. The idea appealed. Muscular legs emerging from half dropped khaki pants, black laced army boots on well-parted feet, the figure bracing itself against the wall. The idea was getting him going again. Jesus, did anyone have sex in any position except standing up these days? Robbo sure as hell didn't. Sex on the run, that was how he had come to expect it.

He cruised past the toilets where the soldiers sometimes fucked late at night. A police car was parked further down the road, supposed to be out of sight. The car was empty. He cruised back in time to see two uniformed officers escorting someone away. He didn't get much of a look at the poor guy. He could see the light reflecting on the police caps as he approached. At least they wore uniforms these days. You stood a better chance that way.

One guy they were leading away. How could one guy be doing anything? It took at least two.

The guy must be being busted for what he was hoping to do. Things hadn't changed that much after all. The police set themselves up. One day, yes one day, it would be the cops, like that poofter-bashing thug in the park a week ago. It happened at Stonewall. It could happen here. Push anyone too far up against the wall and sooner or later they would hit back. Next time it could be a dead cop lying in the park. There would be no surprise witness to come forward then.

Fuck it, Robbo was going to tempt providence and take what came. The fact that he knew that the police were there made it more exciting, more pointed. No one was going to push him into a hunted minority. He was going to fuck to be caught, not to get away with it this time.

He left his bike under a street light and walked up the dark hill, through the park, towards the Memorial. There could have been noises of other couples in the bushes but he wasn't sure. The wind moved the trees up there on the hill. It was the only place in the whole city he had encountered any stirring of air. It drove him on.

He was on the path now. Anyone there would hear him

coming. His boots crunched the gravel. He wasn't sneaking around for anyone. Where had the soldier got to? Robbo couldn't see him.

This time he was going to fuck for equality, fuck to throw off repression. He knew what he wanted to do alright. He wasn't drunk. He'd had two lousy beers. He was making his stand. It had to be with the soldier too. It was time the forces faced the fact that their men fucked each other. Christ, there were even support groups for gay servicemen and yet the forces claimed it didn't exist within their ranks. The Victoria Football League was the same. Gay footballers, you had to be joking! But Robbo had sure been sucked off by quite a few. He was in their line of business.

Now he was on the steps of the mausoleum. No one in sight. He stopped and preened himself in the light. No one came. He walked back down the steps and looked around. He was in full light. Someone should have challenged him if nothing else. What if he had come to desecrate the shrine? How about a blow for men raped in war, eh? That's what he wanted to do. Wank off on the shrine itself.

He walked round the side of the building and back to the other entrance. He heard a noise. His eyes followed the sound. He flashed his lighter. Shit, someone had beaten him to it! There in the darkness of a niche a young soldier was being given a head job by some middle-aged faggot. The soldier still held his bloody rifle as if on duty. His pants were open, not lowered, his cock was being gobbled by some queen, but in all else he was the perfect sentry.

Robbo stomped off through the darkness towards the pool of light where he had left his bike. The fucking pigs wouldn't bust the army, he should have known. Let him get sucked off and then arrest some other guy waiting for the same favour just down the road. So much for his stand for equality! His political statement! Shit, Robbo wasn't political, never had been, just as mad as hell.

He screamed his bike through the still park and headed back through the bright lights over the river. He passed the pissoir where he had seen the young kid at the start of the evening. Outside was another marked police car, empty. The bastards must be trying to close down the whole city. Well, not him. He was going to find himself the hottest, most public place in the city and fuck until he could fuck no more. He wanted to keep going until he couldn't stand up, let alone wank another squirt of juice from his red-sore tool. Shit, he would wank himself all night if need be. And he wasn't going to the saunas or Club 80 to do it. No, he was going to stay out there where he belonged and find sex there the way he always had. The way he had earned the right to.

Who the hell could they have picked up in that cast-iron box? There was only enough room for a single grope and an embarrassed exit. Whoever got touched up unless they wanted it anyway? The whole thing was crazy. Robbo should have dived into the first bog he saw the pigs at, dived in and committed hari-kari. Or better still form his own lynching party. He should go back to one of the bars and get together a party so big they could demolish the pissoir and the pigs inside. But the bar room gays were too interested in what they could line up for the night. If only for once they united, they could outnumber their oppressors and forcibly win back the bogs, their bogs. The beats had always belonged to the queers, so why pretend? What would the pigs achieve by isolated arrests and court appearances? The stupid bastards.

But while Robbo's mind rebelled, his bike bore him further away. Like the others he was in fact bowing to the edict and moving on.

He passed toilet block after toilet block as he did the circuit that night. Action was quiet at first. No one seemed to be on the lookout. Then again he saw a police car. This time it was crawling through the park itself, lights on low. It was like shooters spotlighting for their prey. "One fully grown poof caught blinking in the lights. Get him, mate – and pow." They were still hunted like animals. Who was sick, him or society? Robbo didn't give a fuck how others got their sex – why were they so obsessed with how he got his?

Was all this police activity a reaction to the dead body found in the toilet block? No way. They had never worried before. Trying to find the possible witness? Bullshit. There was no witness. They were just pulling in every poof they could.

And where did he end up? The toilet block where they had left a corpse less than a week before. The scene of their crime, the site where he and five others had struck back. Defiantly he stepped inside. There was no one there. Silent dark walls, a shaft of light from the doorway and the slightly stale smell of urine. Nothing else there at all.

Robbo leant against the wall and gazed into the darkness. Three years on a good behaviour bond the judge had given him. Three fucking years not allowed near this place or any other. Three years for coming here at the age of twenty to find someone to fuck with. Twenty years old and not knowing anywhere else to go. Twenty years old and having to stand up in court on trial for wanting sex with another man. Only twenty years old and your future set out for you because others didn't like your sexual needs. From that age on, having to lie about not having any criminal convictions. A criminal conviction for wanting sex. Not having it – wanting. And now the fuckers were at it again. Eight years later the round-up of the beats was on again. Eight years later and more twenty-year-olds would stand up in court and become outcasts for being found in the bogs. Some like him would plead not guilty only to have their faith in justice quashed. Others, wiser, would quietly plead guilty, pay the fine, carry the stigma and bottle up the rage.

One man in every ten gay. One man in every ten filled with anger, not at their sexuality but at what society forced them to do with it.

And only one corpse in retaliation. So far.

Robbo didn't understand. He wasn't bright, he knew that, but he didn't understand how society could do that to a twenty-year-old. Make him stand up in court guilty until he could prove himself innocent. And how could anyone prove themselves innocent of the intention, the idea, the thought? He wasn't bright, but he was bright enough to know society was screwed up; and each time he broke its taboos, each time he fucked in a toilet block, or on an oval, or in a car park outside in the open – every time he took his revenge. He retaliated every time he jerked off or sucked a cock. He raped the society that had violated his belief in it. The belief of a kid who just thought he might meet someone to get off with.

While he had stood there a figure had come in. He had looked around, then stood at the urinal. As his eyes had become accustomed to the dark, he could see Robbo well. He glanced over but gained no response.

A second figure arrived and took up a stance against the opposite wall. He slouched casually and regarded his colleagues. Then a third arrived and took up a stance at the other end of the urinal. Robbo looked at all three. They were such ordinary men. Just ordinary men like him. Shit, he thought for a moment he was going to cry just looking at the poor bastards.

Then something happened. Two figures at the urinal moved together. The man was no longer leaning on the wall opposite. All three were suddenly together in a tight hard circle, exploring and testing each other for sexual satisfaction. One man was being undressed. Someone was crouching over another's penis. A hand waved to Robbo to join them.

Then there were four men together in the toilet. A montage of hands, mouths, penises. Groping, stroking, sucking, penetrating. Sex was on, the old bog was jumping and Robbo was again making his stand.

Four

In the bedroom Leigh sat before the mirror. He didn't know how long he had been sitting there. It could have been a few hours or even a few days. The absorption held. The obsession was getting worse.

The blinds were drawn and the lamp on the dressing-table threw a funereal light on the pale, waxen face. He gazed intensely at the image reflected there.

He heard the door bang. He didn't move. His eyes remained on the glass. It would only be Prissie returning from her activities. It was nothing to take him away from the dark pupils that stared from the mirror arresting his own. The mirror held his whole world within its bevelled edges. He only lived now before its reflected presence. It was his reality now and nothing would tear him from it, for he had succumbed fully to the escape he had found there. He could share it with no one.

Almost inaudibly he started to recite to the reflection. He spoke slowly, deliberately. It was the confidence of lovers. He smiled contentedly and the image smiled back. Together they lapsed into silence and pondered each other.

Prissie glanced in the mirror in the hallway as she was passing. She was looking pretty tatty these days. Her jaw was still a bit wonky from the week before and the bruised swelling around her left eye remained visible. Perhaps if she hadn't tried to cover it up with make-up at the time, it would have healed sooner and disappeared by now. At least the net disguised it. No one had said anything but she knew it was there. That was what mattered: *she* knew.

"Prissie my girl, you're a mess."

She addressed the mirror quite casually. It was always

Prissie these days. No one much knew her old name. As long as she chose to remember it had always been Prissie. Someone had said it once years back and it had stuck. It suited. She could never decide if it was short for Priscilla, or just descriptive of her manner. By now Prissie was known, an institution. The name had become a person, be it a somewhat tatty one today.

It had been a tiring morning. She had just got back from the dole office. It was her fortnightly visit. Prissie was "unemployable". She had seen her file, it said so. They gave her few hard times at the office. She had been going there so long the people were quite friendly by now. They called her Prissie too.

It wasn't the people that wore her out, it was the public transport. No one ever spoke to her, only about her. It was like wearing a hearing-aid; people assumed she was both deaf and stupid on principle. At least today she had had Leigh's Walkman to block out the world. It alone had made the tram ride possible. On contemplation she decided it probably did look like a hearing-aid peeping out from under the hat. People had thought her disabled. In a way she was.

On the way home she had done the "opportunity" shops. This too was part of the tradition by now. The trouble was there were too many people with money doing them these days. Prissie hadn't bought anything new for years, her budget didn't run to it. Her clothes were culled from those finally rejected by others or handed down by better-off friends. Buying goodwill clothes was often beyond her means now. She always called them "off the peg" clothes. It was just a saying she had affected over the years. Friends all understood what she meant. Leigh called them "pre-worn". He preferred it to the phrase "pre-loved", because it took into account the sweat rings already under the armholes.

But stains and sweat rings didn't worry Prissie. As she always said, "Stains can come and go, but once a cheap chain-store dress, always a cheap chain-store dress."

It was style that mattered more than stains. She could

spot a designer label at one hundred yards and claw her way the width of a church hall in seconds to snatch it up from amid the jumble. Prissie mused to herself. What borax couldn't remove, rhinestones could cover, so nothing "good" was ever too old to be salvaged.

Ask Prissie her favourite designer and she'd say "Schiaparelli".

Ask her favourite shop and she'd say, "St Vincents."

The Salvos were so expensive and the Baptists had no flair. From St Vincents today she had acquired a crêpe de chine with shoulder-pads and also a hat with a wing structure of partridge feathers. The woman there had put the feathers aside especially. She hadn't charged Prissie nearly enough, but Prissie was one of her own special ones in need, on the dole but always so nice.

Prissie took off her hat and coat and tried not to see her disfigured face in the mirror. She took the newly acquired dress to the kitchen and prepared to go over it carefully in the stronger light. It was spread out gently on the kitchen table and each inch perused. Once satisfied she knew the garment thoroughly, she rose and went to the bedroom for disprin.

Leigh was seated at the dressing-table staring into the glass. His hair was gelled out into a bush of fire and his eyes brooded between thick dark lines. He hadn't stirred on her arrival. He didn't speak as she went through the drawers next to him. In the darkened room his body shone as if made of ivory.

"Where the fuck are my disprin?" Prissie asked as she banged through the drawer.

Leigh opened his hand and they were there. He said nothing.

"Thank you," she said pointedly.

She took the box and returned to the kitchen. Placing them in an ashtray, she ground the pills to a powder.

"You haven't any more have you?" she called through.

Leigh didn't answer. She went to the door and stopped.

"Any more, love?"

Leigh turned and finally spoke.

"Has she come?" he asked.
"No love, not yet."
Prissie went into the room and looked at the boy. His skin shimmered, not with the paleness of make-up as she had first thought, but with the excess oil his pores exuded. He had shaken slightly as he spoke, then returned his concentration to the mirror.
"She'll come soon. Come out and help me."
He rose distractedly and moved towards her. She put her arm around him and led him to the kitchen. He sat on an upright chair and gazed at his distorted reflection on the convex surface of the kettle. Prissie continued with her work. She mixed borax with the ground pills and started to paste it onto the armpits of the new dress, working carefully and methodically. For the duration of the chore neither spoke. The paste was then left while she examined the hem and seams carefully, catching up loose ends with a needle and thread as needed. When it met with satisfaction, the dress was finally hand-washed at the sink and placed on a wooden hanger to dry.
Having finished, Prissie held the dress up to inspect her work.
"Stunning, don't you think?"
It dripped onto the spotted floor. Leigh gazed at the kettle.
"I'm scared to hang it outside," Prissie confessed.
She couldn't put anything on the line these days. She had a running battle with the neighbours. It had all started because she moved their washing along one day to make room for her own. Pat had been furious and had just unpegged all Prissie's to let them fall into the dirt. Finding her precious garments in the filth, Prissie had become enraged and banged on Pat's door to confront the bitch. Pat smirked, sympathized, but denied any knowledge. Prissie had left smouldering but unable to prove anything.
It had taken one week for her to retaliate. She waited until the line was full of Pat's lousy wash, then sprayed the lot with dirty water from her upstairs window. She would have used indian ink if she'd had any. It had been rather

fun, she and Leigh playing sniper with water-pistols. She had proved to be a pretty good shot. It was like military training.

Next it had been Pat at the door and Prissie saying, "Oh dear, it must have been the same cretin that dropped mine in the dirt. You can't trust anyone."

Round one to Prissie, but the clothes line was now tempting providence.

"You alright?" she asked.

He gazed ahead.

"Hey. She will come. It's alright."

His eyes locked hers. then his face crumpled.

"I haven't any money," he mouthed helplessly.

Prissie remained quiet. She couldn't help Leigh with money and they both knew it. Anything else but not money. Prissie had only her dole cheque and Leigh's occasional rent money. Leigh's parents gave him the odd handout but that was it for both of them. They were always broke, always on the poverty line. Prissie knew every handout available in the entire inner city area and used them.

When things got desperate for him, Leigh would disappear at night and return hours later with a handful of crumpled notes and a dead expression on his face. Sometimes he returned still broke but smashed out of his mind. It might take days to get him back to normal. Prissie didn't ask how he got that way but she had a good idea. It was none of her business where the money or drugs came from. Likewise Leigh had not asked about her bruised face and jaw. Some old ladies got knocked around all the time and some got paid for it. It was Prissie's concern, not his. Silently he hoped it had paid, to make it worthwhile.

"You arranged for her to come?" Prissie asked.

He nodded.

"And you've got no money?" she continued.

Again he nodded affirmation.

"Shit kid, I'm not going to be here."

And Prissie meant it. If Leigh couldn't pay up, Prissie

wasn't going to stay around to be part of it.

"Sorry, but I'm going out."

He gazed blankly ahead accepting whatever was to come.

Prissie went through to the bedroom and looked at her bruised face. The swelling still showed, giving her eye a Mongolian look. If only it would go down by the weekend. She didn't want all those other gossiping queens knowing. They were all only friends until she turned her back.

Leigh came through to the bedroom and quietly resumed his seat at the dressing-table mirror. He looked intensively into the glass, playing his fingers through his thick oily hair distractedly. His absorption was instant.

Prissie was perturbed. She was going to have to go out again. That meant people, transport, stares. She couldn't cope. Once that day was enough. She gave a sigh. This time it was going to be straight; she didn't have the strength to face the cat calls, the innuendoes, the open abuse. Cursing vocally, she stripped off her clothes and pushed her way to the mirror. She peered at the impasto of make-up on her face.

"It will come off in the shower."

She spoke more to herself than to Leigh. He wasn't listening anyway. Sometimes she wondered why she let the boy stay with her.

Under the shower she watched her long, painted nails play up and down her male loins. She was going to go out straight. She felt like a traitor tricked into betrayal by fatigue. Still, she might even find herself a man.

That was the central problem in her life. Where could she find a man who liked his men to look like women? Gay men had such straight tastes. Their men must be men. Where did that leave her? Hovering as always in the sexual no-man's-land she had occupied since birth. It had made her so old before her time. A fag-hag to other people's affairs while she was in reality still young herself.

She wasn't a woman. She wasn't even a woman inside a man's body. She was just a very effeminate man. Prissie had come to terms with this – why couldn't the rest of the world? She didn't want her body mutilated surgically to become some kind of gross product of science. She wanted to be herself, a man who liked the beautiful things only woman could have. She wanted sequins and feathers and fantasy and style. And also a male lover. It was people who made it so complicated for her. The government labelled her as "unemployable" and filed her away forever to live below the poverty line. Virtually pensioned off by the time she was twenty-one. Others on the dole were hassled to find work: not once did they come up with a single suggestion of work for her.

Yet Prissie was bright, intelligent, in good health and ready to work. She hadn't wanted life in poverty. It had been dished out to her as a cruel by-product of being "too effeminate" to be accepted into the work force. They had even asked her at the Commonwealth Employment Service if she had wanted a sex-change. Perhaps they were offering to pay for it.

Prissie had accepted her sexuality, her desire for style outside that conceived by others, but she couldn't see why she must accept poverty or surgical mutilation. It seemed too high a price to demand.

And the gay men, they oppressed her too. More macho than macho many were these days. Her own kind, who should have tried to understand her, harried and mocked her into assuming another identity not her own amongst them. They assaulted her both verbally and physically until she withdrew and conformed to their image of masculinity in an effort to find a lover. Now she must dress to their tastes and drop her effeminism for the gay world just as she must for the straights. Why couldn't people accept a whole spectrum of sexuality?

What soured her most was that someone somewhere had labelled her as "unfuckable" too. Prissie could enjoy sex just as she could enjoy working, but both were barred from her. It was so fucking unfair. She had a prick just like the others. The only definition of masculinity they could understand was to flaunt that. Prick power. But what of the person inside crying out to be known? What about the renowned Prissie? Did she have to be denied sex?

She sat on the toilet and removed the last of the nail polish with squares of toilet paper dabbed in remover. Nothing effeminate for today. She just wanted to be left alone for a few anonymous hours in the street.

The preparation was the same as she had done a week ago, and look where that had led – a swollen face and back where she started. But Prissie was a fighter and she tried once more. Now all over again she sat in the toilet removing the tell-tale signs from her nails.

She thought of years back, locked in the bathroom with her aunt beating on the door to get in.

"If you're in there Christopher, you open the door this minute."

Prissie frantically washing the lipstick and talcum powder from her face. Her uncle sitting by quietly, quite sure his nephew was locked in the bathroom to masturbate. An ugly collage of scenes culled from the years that had led her here. And for what? To be "unemployable" Prissie?

She rolled the deodorant under her arms, then became aware of the perfume. To make amends she sluiced herself with Leigh's male-oriented aftershave. How she hated it. *Brut* was an apt description. She felt violated by its smell of brilliantine.

She dragged the comb through her wet hair, parting it in a straight line on the left-hand side, then stood back to admire her work. She looked like Hitler without the moustache. She dragged her hand through it to soften the effect. The make-up around her eyes was too ingrained to be moved by soap and water alone, but the residue was so slight it would pass. Besides, Prissie wouldn't recognise herself absolutely free of make-up. She would feel naked.

In the bedroom she rummaged through the cupboard and emerged with strangely patched jeans and an old blue check shirt in winceyette. From Leigh's drawer she borrowed a pair of jockettes. She put them on. They felt awkward. Shrugging, she continued to dress. The jeans were a little too snug. The shirt she wore with the collar turned up. It looked wrong but she didn't know why. It looked a little as if she was auditioning for principal boy in Peter Pan.

After much effort she found matching socks – bright blue – a pair of high-heeled cowboy boots and a duffle coat. She dithered over the coat, then decided it wasn't cold enough to warrant it. Standing back and looking in the mirror, it didn't look too bad.

"What you think?" she asked Leigh.

His eyes shifted in the mirror from his reflection to hers. He nodded. Prissie beamed and pushed him on the shoulder.

"Thanks kid," she preened and waltzed out.

She still had no idea where she was going but took the extra butch precaution of rolling up the last of her banknotes and thrusting them into her money pocket.

Wow, it felt good. Prissie was off. Maybe for a cruise, maybe just to get out of the house, but she was feeling high and anything could happen.

When she hit the street she started to have reservations. She wafted *Brut* but minced self-consciously. She ventured a few yards, then stopped. People were staring, something was wrong. What if she saw someone she knew? What if they saw her? The uneasiness started to set in. If only she could go back, but she couldn't. She tried again. She walked along too fast to look in the shop windows. She walked as if with a sense of purpose she didn't feel, for there was no purpose. She had no idea where she was going.

The shopping area was small. Once down each side and she was sure people were starting to look. She tried the Save the Children shop. The sign on the door said it was open. It was closed. Back up on the same side of the road. Nothing to do.

She sauntered towards the underground toilets submerged in the middle of the intersection. Surely that would occupy some time. The steps smelt as she went down between the railings. At least it was a change to go into the Men's unchallenged. Her disguise was working that far.

Inside it was like a rabbit warren lined in stained yellow tiles. It offended her aesthetically. Illegible graffiti scarred the woodwork. A chain clanged. The thud of its heavy metal handle reverberated as a cistern flushed reluctantly. At the bottom of the steps she stopped. Someone pushed past her and out, nearly knocking her off her feet. She smelt garlic and diesel oil. Her nose screwed up involuntarily.

There was a scuffling sound from the washroom. Two heavily set men, one in a tracksuit, looked out at her. The other was going bald. He looked at Prissie, spat on the ground and turned away. Prissie feigned disinterest and loitered near the entrance. The heavier man in the tracksuit continued to give the other a head job. He slobbered noisily. They took no notice of Prissie at all. Prissie hovered, then faltered a step nearer. It was hardly romantic but it would do. The balding man held onto the other's shoulders and thrust his head back. His eyes fell on Prissie. She smiled, expecting an invitation to join in. He narrowed his eyes. "Piss off," he hissed.

He jerked his fist and elbow in an obscene gesture Prissie knew well. The other didn't even pause in his activity.

She scuttled back up the steps into the stark daylight. Trying to regain some dignity, she continued her saunter she knew not where. It had given her quite a turn, not good for her nerves or morale.

Venturing a block further, she browsed past a sex shop. The windows were painted over and the door barred by western-style saloon doors. Summoning up courage she pushed through. The doors sprang shut behind her like a trap and she was there inside. Worried faces glanced up as magazines snapped shut. Prissie took in the scene as well as she could, then headed down one side to the magazines with titles she knew dimly. Her eyes ran along the glossy pictures sealed safely inside plastic covers. Above the magazines an array of leather hoods, flimsy leather belts, chains and armlets were displayed. There was also an unlikely sized black leather jock-strap.

Her eyes turned. From the counter opposite a dildo as large as a table lamp flaunted itself amid the other wares. An inflated doll, gasping mouth, no hands or feet, spread its legs above the door. A cardboard sign pointing to the backroom proudly read "Videos".

Prissie's eyes fell to the glass-topped counter and its array of boxes and jars.

"If you want me to show you anything, just ask," the man behind the counter offered.

Prissie nodded and continued to gaze around awkwardly.

"We've got all kinds of panties and things for you or your girlfriend," the guy said helpfully, indicating a board of tawdry crotchless knickers.

"Thank you," Prissie said and swallowed.

"Gay selection over to the back," he added.

Trying one last time, Prissie puffed up her chest, clamped her chin to her throat and saying in her butchest voice, "Thank you mate", walked out through the door.

She strode with her feet pointed out and her knees slightly bent, her hands thrust into her front pockets. Two paces down the street and someone whistled. Catcalled was more accurate. Someone catcalled her there for all to see. It was no good, she fooled no one. It just didn't feel right. It just wasn't Prissie.

She caught a tram and crossed the city. No one sat next to her. The man opposite looked away for the entire journey. He had big balls; they sat splayed on the seat forcing his legs apart like a frog. Why couldn't Prissie sit like that? She tried, then gave up and crossed her legs tightly at the knee. She played with her nails, scratchingoff the remnants of polish she found there. Finally the balls hauled themselves into an upright position and got off the tram. Only seated were they so visible. When the man stood they disappeared under the shadow of his stomach.

Prissie remained on the tram stop after stop. At least nobody wolf-whistled her on the tram.

Outside the hospital a woman got on with a small child.

It was an overweight girl of about six. At sixteen she would look like her mother. They sat together in the seat vacated opposite her. The child was learning to speak French and repeated phrases parrot fashion after her mother as she crawled across the seat and tried to look out through the window.

Prissie thought of Leigh. She felt guilty running out on him to face the music alone. He was her boy. She felt responsible for him. Perhaps he would be alright. Maybe the deal wouldn't come anyway.

Maybe they would accept payment later. Maybe he could screw for the stuff instead. Jayne had always had a pretty insatiable appetite in that direction. It wouldn't be the first time Leigh had hawked his body. Prissie had never shared it, but others had, for a price. Why did she let him stay?

The child opposite bounced up and down chanting, "Je m'appelle Gabrielle" and laughing all the while.

Her mother smiled indulgently. Others smiled and listened in.

"Such a bright child," a woman opposite observed to her companion.

The mother smiled as if she had been awarded a ribbon for horse-breeding.

The child laughed and started to crawl across to the seat beside Prissie. Prissie smiled down. The mother pulled the child back guardedly.

"No dear, stay with me."

The woman and her companion nodded wisely. Prissie decided to leave the tram.

She alighted from the tram and crossed the road. She peered into the chemists to see the clock. A girl in a white uniform peered curiously back. It was still early yet. She hoped Leigh was alright.

Another block of shops to browse past. Prissie thought she spied an "op" shop. Eagerly she crossed the road. It was only a dry cleaners. She caught sight of herself in a flaking mirror on the shopfront. Curiously the swelling didn't look as out of place with the cheap check shirt.

People would put it down to rough trade if they bothered to think at all. Usually they didn't. At least it stopped her being sexless. In a way she kind of liked it. It gave her status.

And that night, the other men had accepted her then. She had been one of them when it came to the blow. There had been no division then. She had been one of them unquestioned by all. The unity, that was what it had meant to her most of all. A conspiracy of men against men.

The smell of coffee greeted her nostrils. Suddenly she decided she needed the caffeine. The need gnawed at her insides crying out for satisfaction and she answered it. Pushing open the door of the coffee shop she stepped inside on her cowboy heels and took a seat at the counter. It felt more European to sit there, far more cosmopolitan, than sitting at one of the tables. Ignoring the fact that the woman called her "love", she ordered a short black. Nothing parochial about her.

"There you are, young man," the woman announced, placing the small glass before her.

Prissie grew two inches on the stool. "Young man", that was more like it.

A man came and sat two seats away. He had moved from one of the small tables further back. She smiled at him. He looked confused. Her mistake. He ordered a capucino. Breakfast coffee, she thought contemptuously to herself. She took a swallow of her espresso and it nearly took her breath away. Tears burnt in her eyes as she tried not to gasp. Please God, don't let anyone see.

"You feeling alright?"

The man leant forward with concern.

"Just period pains," Prissie gasped back, then went crimson at what she had said and choked some more. Messed things up again no doubt.

He laughed.

"Have some mineral water," he suggested.

He ordered and ministered the elixir. Prissie thanked him, fighting both for breath and dignity.

He seemed disposed to chat. He wasn't really her type but Prissie felt obliged to be polite. It was pleasant but banal. Two strangers exchanging civilities, nothing more. She didn't realise it was a pick-up until he prepared to leave.

"Perhaps I could see you again," he suggested.

He handed her a card. It said he was an insurance salesman. Prissie let him pay for the coffee and kept the card until he had left the shop. When she left, it remained behind on the counter. Not really her type.

She continued down the street but her ego was rebuilding. She minced with confidence. No need to try out her seaman's roll now. Her heels rapped out their precise, fast rhythm as she proceeded on her way.

She wondered about the time. Just a little longer. Soon she could return to see what was left of Leigh, her silly, pretty boy.

To kill the hours, she popped into a department store to price sequins for à repair job. Lattice patterns of beading over gin stains could work wonders. Clattering past people on the up escalator, she knew heads were turning but it no longer mattered. Her disguise was up, she was bored with it. Let heads turn in acknowledgement as she passed; hundreds of people would give anything for just that attention.

At the top of the escalator she turned right, past the headless tailor's dummies. They all stood in a row waiting to have their bust sizes adjusted by anyone willing to turn a little wheel. It all seemed rather brazen to Prissie. Haberdashery. This was officially a woman's world, hallowed ground untrod by male feet. Prissie breezed through confidently. Knowing eyes marked her progress.

She considered a browse through the dress patterns but decided it wasn't worth the detour. Nothing ever corresponded to her size anyway. Instead she drifted through the fabric section touching here and there to assess quality. It was true, they really didn't make fabrics like they used to. All these poor quality synthetics with print out of line with the weave of the fabric. If you cut along the printed lines you ended up anywhere, half on the cross with gathers just where you didn't need them. You had to go pre-War for real quality. Linens and cottons were almost unobtainable now. It was like trying to buy sheets that weren't polyester. No, quality had gone by the wayside.

She pondered long and hard at the sequin counter, managing to slip a self-cover button set into the front of her shirt. The card sat close to her body and hardly showed at all. She purchased a metre and a half of black sequins and watched them being placed into a small white bag. Only yards from the counter she presented the receipt to one of the dummies, and slipped the button card in with the sequins. The bag was proof of purchase; loss of receipt was understandable.

As she turned to descend the escalator a figure rushed up behind her and grabbed her shoulder. Prissie nearly jumped through the roof. All for a card of buttons – Christ, she'd give them back, anything, just let her go. Prissie had never been in trouble with the police before. She had no record. They would have to let her go; it was her first offence. Please be merciful.

"Just the person I wanted to see," a voice said. "How long can you spare?"

She stared startled at a face she barely recognised. "Pardon?"

The face smiled encouragingly. She sort of remembered him; at least she hoped she did, if it meant she wasn't going to be placed behind bars.

"Please – Prissie, isn't it? Can you spare the time to give me a hand? I don't know what I'm doing."

"Sure," she replied uncertainly.

That face, where was it from?

"I've got this pattern for a pullover and no one will help me buy the wool."

He looked pretty desperate.

"Please?"

His look implored more than his words could.

"Come on," she said, and grabbing him by the arm, she marched determinedly towards the wool section.

"Now, where's your pattern?" she demanded.

He unfolded a small booklet from his back pocket and smiled weakly.

"Which one?" she demanded.

The book was ceremoniously opened to the middle page where a youth smiled back in stripes.

Prissie took the pattern and scanned the instructions.

"This way." She handed the book back and set off through the labyrinth of counters to the range of the correct yarns.

"What colours do you want?"

"I don't know." He hesitated. "Something different from those."

She ran her eyes expertly along the wall and pointed out which bundles to choose from.

"Is that all?" he asked.

Together they eyed the photograph and then the wool before them.

"Looks like it"

"Isn't it awful? No one will help you," he started, but it was too late. Prissie had marched off again, this time to consult with the saleswoman. She came back and informed him, "That's all they've got. Give me the pattern."

He stood looking uneasy. They were the only men in the entire department. He was becoming acutely embarrassed. Prissie watched him slyly from the corner of her eye. She could dimly recollect where they had met before.How did he know she could knit? she wondered.

"I hate it here," he confessed.

"Nonsense," she snapped, "it's going to be fun." Then to be helpful she added, "You can use any eight-ply you know. It's all the same."

"Oh."

He looked sheepish. "I don't know if it's worth going through with it."

"We are not leaving till we have what you want."

And it was on. Like the Red Queen she snatched up his hand and they were off again on their race against time. Together they charged through the department pulling out packets of wool here, odd balls there, checking for ply and colour and discarding them again in a topsy-turvy, multi-coloured trail. Women stopped amazed at this invasion of their domain but Prissie was relentless: the path she left, a faultline.

Finally they found what she considered the best: pure wool and on special.

"Now how many balls do you want?"

He felt the whole floor was listening. He whispered his requirements hoarsely.

The balls had all been separated by previous shoppers. It was really a counter of oddments. Sealed packets of two or three balls, odd ones coming unwound: Prissie was in her element. They started to turn them over. Prissie paused.

"What's your name?" she asked suddenly.

"Geoff," he replied self-consciously.

"Geoff, that's right. Now you find what colours you want and I'll match them up."

Through the turmoil he moved quickly, settling for the main colour at speed. She showed him how to match for shade and dye lot. He tried to obey but was scolded for digging out an odd ball that was unlabelled.

Two other women began to sift through the wool also. Geoff and Prissie became separated, both engrossed in the same task.

"How about this for contrast?" she called and tossed a ball high over the table for him to catch. He caught it high in the air and grinned back. The two other fossickers looked surprised.

"Too bright," he called back and returned it the same way. "I'm really very quiet."

"Rubbish," Prissie replied and threw a second ball just to show.

By now the shop assistant was looking worried and making little unsure movements towards them.

"This one," Geoff announced, pulling out a light yellow.

"How many?" Prissie demanded.

He consulted the book. "Four," he checked, and they

went back to work. They located three. One to go and they were finished.

"Excuse me," said a heavy voice.

Prissie turned and looked. A young Italian woman was addressing her.

"How many balls please for a child?"

"What?" Prissie queried.

"How many balls please for a child's jumper?"

Geoff laughed. Prissie couldn't see why. She looked at the infant with the woman.

"Four or five," she snapped and returned to work.

"She thinks you work here," Geoff confided.

Prissie shrugged and returned to her chore of pawing through the oddments.

Finally they triumphed and carried their selection to the counter. The assistant looked relieved and even managed a subdued smile.

"Needles?" Prissie demanded.

"I think I've got them," Geoff replied.

"You've knitted before," Prissie announced.

The girl started to ring up the cash register.

"Don't forget your tension check. It's necessary when you use a different wool. But you probably know."

He shook his head.

"Thanks," he said, and looked embarrassed.

They paid the girl and received the package. Geoff looked plain relieved. Prissie looked exuberant. At the top of the escalator they stopped to part company. Geoff made a little speech. He said, "I would never have done it on my own. I would have died."

"That's alright," said Prissie.

She carefully extracted a paper bag from her back pocket and removed a card of strange-looking buttons. To Geoff's surprise she ceremoniously presented them to a gold mannequin draped in red tartan, and embarked onto the down-escalator.

She waved him off in the street saying, "Let me know how it turns out."

If only she could be sure where she had met him before.

It showed how far and wide the name of Prissie had spread.

Outside the street was getting darker and crowded. It must be nearly late enough for her to go home.

She thought how nice people could be, as she walked along the street. Really, it took so little to restore one's faith. Less than an hour ago she had been pretty down in the dumps. All it had taken to lift her out of it was for a strange man to buy her a cup of coffee and someone to need her help buying wool. It had confirmed to herself that there was something she was good at. Something that she had or knew that others wanted. Playing butch had nearly ruined the afternoon. It was the real Prissie that had thrown wool around so joyously in Myers or picked up an insurance man over coffee. Sitting there with her knees crossed and her finger pointed as she held her glass, that was Prissie. Denim or blue check didn't make the man. She was successful for what came from within, and hopeless when pushed to conform.

She touched her face. She had quite forgotten the swelling there. It hadn't affected the afternoon much at all. Now she was glad she had stirred from the flat and ventured further into the world. The shadow of last Friday's exprience need not cloud her future.

And what a strange experience it had been, for that too had been pure Prissie. That too had come from deep inside herself. It hadn't shocked her at the time – why should it now? She felt in a way that she had almost initiated the incident as well as being there for the culmination.

Now, now it was time to go home to Leigh. Ten to one she would find him still locked before the mirror, bedraggled tights and matted hair. How she envied and loved that mass of hair. How she loved that messed-up boy. Crazy wasn't it, but Prissie loved the fact that he needed her.

The tram stop was now crowded and she had to jostle with the crowds to even get on. No chance of a seat at this time of night. How she disliked these new trams. On the old ones you could avoid paying at peak hours. So much for progress! She stood sandwiched between office workers with bored, blank faces. They shuffled aimlessly along the carriage at each new stop, allowing more and more bodies to be packed on. No one spoke or smiled or even looked at each other. The exit doors were clogged up, the windows shut, the carriage airless. Prissie longed for the Walkman. Rush hour trams were more impersonal than those she usually rode but no more pleasant. She would be glad when the ride was over.

A few people gradually got off, stop by stop. The crowd thinned. It became more bearable. Then at the hospital they packed on more than ever. By now Prissie was packed into the end of the carriage. She still hadn't managed to get a seat.

Rather than stay on the tram any longer than absolutely necessary, Prissie decided to walk the last couple of stops. Getting off the tram, she regretted the decision not to wear the duffle coat, it was so cold. She hurried towards home unsure what would await her there. Leigh would be in – he never left the flat these days – but in what state would she find him, that was the problem. She really couldn't cope with ministering to someone else's wounds and broken bones. Her own caused her enough concern.

She could just envisage another night in the casualty department. A seat of dumb, worried faces opposite and nurses smirking away behind the reception desk. The same old torn magazines and stale, warm food from the vending machines to keep you awake. Day dawning through the plate glass doors as the last of the wheelchairs and stretchers streamed in.

Seven o'clock in the morning and still waiting because you were not regarded as an emergency. Going home eventually unattended. Perhaps rest and your own GP were the answer. Swelling and bruising that lasted into the week and no one had got around to telling you why.

Why was Leigh so stupid as to set himself up like this? No more stupid than she had been. What if the police had done the rounds of the hospitals making enquiries and found Prissie sitting there waiting for attention? She hadn't thought clearly. She wondered what had become of the other men.

She turned into their street and her thoughts returned to the present. She could see the flat from the street, but because Leigh had all the blinds closed there was no sign of life, no way of telling if life still existed inside. A brief desire to procrastinate longer, then she overcame it and continued briskly forward towards the darkened building that was home.

Going up the stairs she thought she could hear the faint sound of music. The stairwell could play tricks on you and make it unclear which flat the sounds were coming from.

She opened the door. The warm, soft air and music hit her together. Whatever had happened, it was alright. She stepped inside. In the hallway she took a few deep breaths just to be prepared, then she proceeded into the lounge. She stopped in the doorway.

Leigh looked at her with a glazed smile. He was sitting on the floor playing with a tin box full of buttons. On his head he wore a set of plastic Mickey Mouse ears someone had given him months beforehand. On the floor with him crawled a filthy child. Prissie looked at them both. Leigh beamed as if at some profound achievement.

"Hi," he said, "we've been waiting for you."

"She came," Prissie observed.

"Yeah. We've got Laurie 'cause I couldn't pay."

Prissie laughed and came forward. "We've got Laurie" – it meant *she* had him to mind. In no time Leigh would be right out of it and lose all interest. Then it would be up to her as usual. She hated to think how many times the poor child had been dumped on her in the past. Jayne only kept him because it meant she got a single mother's pension and everyone in the department kept off her back about not working. He would now stay with Prissie until one day when Jayne would swoop down and reclaim him as a long lost weapon against the welfare officers. The poor kid.

Prissie would have kept him permanently if she only could. Adopt him, run away with him, what did it matter if only he could become hers? She just couldn't see a way to achieve it.

"Hello darling," she said, squatting on the floor next to him.

The child turned and gurgled recognition. Prissie seized him up in a great bearhug, rocking in the sheer pleasure of holding him. The child held on. He always remembered Prissie. She was his surrogate mother. She had looked after him when he had come out of hospital. Only she understood his fear of water, his need to be held so tight. Others, specialists, said he was retarded. She knew better He was her baby.

Leigh sat by contentedly and continued to let the buttons play through his hands.

"Don't you lose any," Prissie observed.

They were for her dressmaking. Later she would add the new sequins to the tin. Leigh smiled up at her vaguely. It had all sorted itself out well. He articulated, "See, I'm happy, you're happy, it's all fine."

Yes, all was fine. His eyes wore their familiar unnatural, contented glaze and the heat within his veins bore out his fantasies.

Leigh and Laurie, Prissie's two children. Prissie, mother of two. One was retarded, one would be dead at twenty-five. She wiped the thought from her mind.

"Have you eaten?" she asked Leigh for both of them. He shook his head but seemed unsure.

Prissie still held the baby in her arms. She rose to her feet, then held him out to look at him more clearly. Poor kid was filthy. The remains of something dark and sticky still stained his face around his mouth. She hoped it was only chocolate. One of his shoes was missing and he smelt distinctly of shit.

"Let's clean you up, precious," Prissie cooed.

The child dribbled in response. She took it as consent.

It was time to go into action. How could people let kids get into such a state? Jayne was hopeless and Leigh little better either. It was just laziness. They were a couple of sluts, nothing more. Jayne would now be off fucking some unfortunate eighteen-year-old who would still have to pay for his deal of dope. Leigh would shortly be in the land of the pixies and no good to anyone. The only difference was that Jayne would go on fucking young boys well into her forties, probably die with her legs in the air, while Leigh would one day descend into the land of the pixies never to re-emerge.

This was a fact that Prissie had to keep a firm hold on. No matter how much she loved him, he was a lost cause. And Prissie would remain loyal until the end.

A soft humming came from her lips as she carried Laurie to the kitchen. Perhaps she enjoyed tragedy. Let's face it, she was a collector of stray dogs and derelicts. The small affection she felt returned was reward enough. "Unemployable", "unfuckable"; but Prissie was doing what she did best.

On the laminex table in the kitchen, she sat the child to undress him. She removed the super-butch roll-necked sweater Jayne had dressed him in. Who else would dress an infant in jeans and a fishermans knit when there were such nice things around for the picking? That woman had no sense of style.

When she removed his vest, she saw the yellow of the fading bruises beneath. She closed her mind off, she didn't want to know. She thought of the woman on the tram and her fat, healthy child reciting its meaningless French. That child was so lucky. And the woman too. People spoke to you when you had a child.

The nappy was of course soiled. It hadn't been changed for hours and had chaffed at his legs and bottom. It was one of those awful disposable pads that were neither absorbant nor disposable. Slow incineration was about the only way of getting rid of them. You couldn't drop them in the garbage and they refused to flush away down the toilet. She had seen Jayne once in frustration hurl one from the window of a moving car. That was the closest thing to style that the kid's mother had ever experienced.

Laurie had his own special clothes that Prissie kept for him when he visited her. They were kept hidden away – good, old fashioned nappies and lovely little linen dresses.

He was such a pretty child when he stayed with Prissie. Such wonderful things culled from "op" shops and restored lovingly by hand to pristine condition. Darned, stitched, starched – no child could ask for more. Gainsborough would have painted the child when Prissie had finished with him.

She bathed him in the kitchen sink. Because of his fear of water, she could only use a few inches at a time. It meant changing the water several times but was worth it. Laurie stood through the whole operation, his hands gripping onto Prissie's shoulders as she stood facing him. Such a solemn, trusting little face he had. No one could say her baby was retarded. It had just been the shock that was all. His physical development was back to normal. True, he was small for his age – but retarded, no. He knew his Prissie. He knew he was safe once he made it to her.

Drying and powdering him, she again noted the tell-tale signs of the week's abuse. Why the fuck couldn't Jayne leave him alone?

She secured his nappy, slid on the plastic pants and sat him upright. Lots of chidlren still needed nappies at his age. He had almost been out of them when the accident had occurred. Soon he would be ready to try and discard them again. It just required time and patience. "Accident," Prissie thought. If only she had been there that day, Jayne would never have got away with it. One day Jayne would get hers, there were enough people willing it. But at present Laurie's needs must come first. Prissie was needed.

He sat patiently as she carefully brushed his fine wispy hair. He was so solemn. Such a vain little queen really. She wondered what he would be like when he grew up. If he would reject her along the way. At this age children were so accepting but later, in adolesence, she didn't like to predict.

Then it was through to play in the warm with Leigh until they had selected his clothes for the evening. Leigh was setting out buttons in a pattern before him. He smiled but said nothing. Laurie snuggled happily into the warm hollow between his knees and seemed oblivious to the lack of attention that Leigh displayed.

In the bedroom Prissie opened "Laurie's drawer". She rested her eyes on the neatly folded clothes. They all looked so tiny. Tiny little pairs of socks, scrubbed and darned; little jackets; overalls; and the favourite: a little gingham smocked dress in blue and white. Prissie lifted it out. Hours of work someone had put into this little creation. White silk threads, blue ribbons, minute puff sleeves with a white lace edging. Prissie could have hugged the garment, it held so much love, but she didn't want to crease it. She carefully selected matching socks, a clean vest and even slippers. Her baby was going to look special, he *was* special. She wanted to stay with him, see him grow up, see how handsome he became.

She wondered if he would be straight or take after her. Would he always be pretty and so, so accepting? As long as he didn't turn out like that boy in the park. He could reject her, that was one thing, but as long as he never became a bigoted thug to abuse her. But he wouldn't, not her Laurie.

Finally dressed in all his glory, he was again entrusted to Leigh's care, to have his finger-nails painted. It was a painstaking effort that required all their concentration. The more out of it Leigh became, the more he laughed as he met Laurie's solemn gaze, as the tiny bobs of colour took their place on the little nails. Laurie knew to keep his hands still and the effort was enormous.

Prissie took one last look at her family and went into the kitchen. Tomorrow they would have to get some proper food. Tonight it was too late, there was nothing. In desperation she decided on custard. It was the only thing she had that he would be able to eat. She searched the cupboards for fruit or something to add to it, but in vain. They had a small amount of white bread. Cut fine that would do for breakfast but tonight it was just custard.

When she returned to the lounge, Leigh was asleep on the floor amid the buttons. Laurie sat there, a large plastic button in his mouth. She took it away and together they sat there before the heater, eating bowls of warm, sticky custard.

Five

As he went through the double doors into the gym, the noise and smell of the aerobics class hit him full on. Until that moment Tony had been all geared up for a hard workout. His resolve started to wane. It had been a hard week, one of the hardest he could remember. He had planned to put his body through its paces, work up a sweat and clear the load off his mind.

Before him a motley sea of leotards bent and stretched no longer in unison. The music pounded out its beat; most of them had lost it long before. They were on the last frantic dash before the winding down stage. He only just had time to change.

He slipped past the desk and to the changing-rooms. A wall of lockers and none of them spare. He changed hastily and emerged ready to go. The music had finished but the earlier class were still in place stretching and cooling off.

In a small space at the side of the room he did a few warm-up exercises, then a little bar work. He had to prepare like this beforehand or he would be hopeless. He eyed the previous class casually. Most of his class would just walk on and off with no preparation. He couldn't do it that way. He looked around at the others patiently waiting for the next session. Reflected in the mirrored wall there appeared to be thousands of them. Once again he tried to muster the desire to go through with it. Competition was one incentive, but this was an easy bunch. With any luck they would get one of the women who really put them through the works. That was what he needed, someone else to provide the will-power and he could then follow, his mind disconnected from his body.

He and Mark had been coming here for about twelve months. Now he came alone. His body was fitter than it had ever been. His mind was bombed out on valium at "his own discretion". That's what the bottle said. The doctor had been wonderful through it all. God knows how he would have got through it without him. It was so easy to see how people had crushes on their doctors. At times Tony's was the only person he knew who seemed to care. He even knew when to make a joke of it and when there were signs that it was getting serious. Because their relationship was too important, Tony would have to ween himself off it. Consultations had better be out for a week at least, he decided. Tonight he would even resist the temptation to phone the surgery to listen to the recorded message the doctor left there. No, tonight it would be exercise. He always had the valium for later if it got tough. Anyway, Peter would call.

Peter had phoned just about every night that week so he had no reason to believe tonight would be the exception. The guy was keen, you had to admit that. He had worn down Tony's resistance until finally he had agreed to go over for dinner on the Saturday night and still he wouldn't let up. He would phone again tonight.

Tony slid his foot along the polished wooden bar one last time, then returned to an upright and lifted his leg down, shaking it loose. He repeated the exercise on the other side, then waited quietly for the previous class to finish up. The silence was as striking as the previous din had been. Now a lone voice issued calmly through the system telling the masses to relax. Relax they did – not a stir. The voice stopped, then spoke one last command.

Suddenly it was over and there was a mad rush for positions in the next class. Most stampeded for the back, Tony stepped to the front where he had a better view in the mirrors. Here he could check his own contortions. Staring into the mirror he tried isolating his rib-cage and moving it from side to side. He met with little success. It occupied the few spare minutes until the class would start. To the others it looked pretentious but he had to do something. He couldn't just sit like the others. He didn't like coming here alone. It felt uncomfortable. If it came to that, he didn't like going anywhere alone. He didn't like living alone. He had no choice. That wasn't strictly true. The rate Peter was coming on . . . But he didn't want Peter.

The trouble was going anywhere, doing anything he and Mark had previously done together. To do it alone seemed to be parading some kind of failure. Failure to hold onto a lover. It sounded nothing, but he smarted under the humiliation and needed the valium to shut out the knowing eyes and quick exchange of looks of those around him.

Everyone knew Mark had left him. Everyone knew he was alone not by choice but by failure. The most ordinary people could hold onto a relationship, yet here he was alone because he couldn't.

His doctor had seen the collapse of it coming for months. He himself hadn't. It had genuinely taken him by surprise. All the friends and acquaintances who phoned to say they had seen it coming just made it worse. They didn't understand. He didn't want to hear anyone running down Mark, he just wanted him back.

He had done some stupid things in the past couple of weeks. Accepting that lift from Peter had been one of them. Going out at all last Friday had been one big mistake. He should have gone straight home from the gym and called it a night. It was just that the flat wasn't home to him right now and he didn't want to be there. He put off the homecoming as long as possible. A homecoming to an empty flat was no homecoming at all.

An instructor he hadn't seen before was taking the platform and preparing for his period of rule. He snapped a set of red wrist bands into place, leant forward to the microphone and introduced himself. Tony didn't listen for the name; he wasn't interested.

The music started. They did some basic breathing and a few very orthodox stretching exercises. Tony watched the instructor mark them, then watched himself in the mirror as he repeated them. It all seemed pretty elementary but he persevered. The first track came to a end and they were getting nowhere. The second track started. Would you believe more breathing, then arm exercises? Finally the legs came in too as they paced back and forward punching into mid-air. Tony watched the mock aggression reflected in his face and wondered how it had looked that night one week before. Had his face reflected the real anger pent up inside him, or worn this same mask?

Legs apart, they were now touching alternate toes and the instructor was looking pretty puffed. Tony watched carefully and saw that the guy was now only marking it approximately, while he himself achieved an easy, graceful swing.

Time for the run and the instructor was clearly not doing well. He kept them at a moderate jog with a few awkwardly executed hops and skips thrown in. Even Mark could do better than that and he was notorious for taking it easy, wisecracking away at the front, and shortcutting anything difficult. Tony felt like walking out of the class there and then. With an effort he made himself stay. He looked around. No one else seemed dissatisfied with the proceedings; it must just be the mood he was in tonight.

Returning to their places, they rested flat on their backs and did more breathing exercises to prepare for the stomach and thigh work. When they did eventually get started it was a walkover for Tony. He could do these until the end of the lesson if necessary. He watched his reflection in the side mirror then looked back to the instructor. Tony was clearly doing a better job himself.

When they finally slid their legs apart, Tony went right down into the splits; the instructor did not. From then on Tony stubbornly did his own thing right there in the front. It was soon noticed. The instructor started to give him worried sidelong glances. He continued to work independently. Then for the second run, Tony went off and showered. As a workout it had been a write-off. As an ego boost it was of slight help. As a distraction to the week's problems, it had served little good at all.

Outside in the brisk air he started the slow walk towards home. He was in no hurry so could afford to walk slowly. The more time it occupied, the better. It would mean less time to endure at home.

Always in the past they'd had Mark's car, now he felt marooned in the flat without transport. It was just one of many ways in which his life had changed. Once home, he would be isolated, with just the phone to needle him into expectation.

Peter would try the number just once more. Really Tony should be home by now. He went to the gym on a Friday but should finish that by about six. Peter wanted to be sure about Saturday evening. After all, if he was going to go to that much trouble, he wanted to be sure the boy would turn up.

He switched down the sound on the television and arose from the deep blue armchair. Straightening the cushion, he crossed the room and went out to the hallway to telephone. There was no need to look in his monogrammed leather book; he knew the number by now. He had always had a methodical mind and remembered telephone numbers easily. It was only a matter of a few minutes concentrated rote-learning and they were there permanently for recall. He dialled and waited.

Again there was no answer. He replaced the receiver and look critically at the instrument. He really must get a touch-phone; this model was so superseded that it was becoming an embarrassment. On Monday he would get one of the girls at work to place an order for him. Now who did he know at Telecom who could arrange for it to be installed as a priority?

Surveying the hall critically, he wondered if his cleaning lady was being paid too much. Her ironing was good, he never had any complaints about the freshly laundered shirts that bore witness to her industry – but her cleaning! It wasn't as if she had any excuse. He always made sure everything was neatly in place before he went to bed the night before, so her job would be straightforward when she arrived the next morning. In addition he didn't like the idea of her prying. He'd had to compromise his privacy to have her there at all. But no one did their own cleaning these days and his friends would think him either too mean or hard up if he didn't employ someone.

What he really needed was a well-trained house-boy to live in. That would be status! When he had first met Anh, he had considered the possibility, but as he got to know the boy, he hadn't proved suited at all - very lazy and quite without morals. Any other refugee boy would have counted his blessings. A good home in a rich country, what more did the boy want?

With Tony he would be able to keep the cleaning woman and allow the boy free reign in the second bedroom. Tony seemed honest, clean, reliable. It would leave only the small third room for visitors, but then he wanted to discourage staying guests. It was hard to put up with other people in his house. People who didn't know how to stack the dishwasher or insisted on using the ashtrays and then left them sitting around reeking their foul odours.

Returning to the lounge, he folded the day's newspaper to the page of the crossword and tried again to complete it. The thing usually exasperated him because the clues were so inexact. Often he felt like challenging the accuracy of the solutions. In addition his own writing displeased him. The carefully jotted letters always looked haphazard against the straight lines of the print. It was perturbing to associate them with his own love of order;

There were a few things about this new boy Tony that worried him. He was an untidy dresser and rather casual in manner. What pleased Peter most was Tony's body. It was well exercised, trained, kept in order, and that Peter respected.It was something he himself hadn't attained. His own sense of order collapsed when it came to his body. The demands of his social and work life didn't allow him to utilize his own gold-pass membership to the executive gym. Groomed a little, Tony would be quite presentable in most circles. His speech was good, his background would, Peter was sure, prove to be adequate. Anyway, having something a little "Bohemian" was quite acceptable these days. Tony could be Peter's little eccentricity. The little touch of the unpredictable that made all else in his life reflect its own perfect order. In fact, Peter wouldn't be surprised if secretly he liked the excitement of having that little something different from all his friends.

He looked at the crossword again. He had gone wrong: "pitch" was supposed to be "toss" not "tone". Erasing was impossible on newspaper so he would now have to abandon the project altogether. Fancy a crossword in a paper of that calibre resorting to slang terms like that. In one way he was glad he hadn't got it right; it would have reflected poorly if he had.

Carefully placing the pen on the side-table, he carried the paper to the rubbish disposal in the kitchen and placed it in the section for dry garbage. He then fastidiously washed and dried his hands before taking down a recipe book to consult for the next evening. Peter didn't like chances, so he turned to the chapter on dinner parties for two. He would use one of the menus complete. After all, the balance would be better that way than chopping and changing into some mishmash of a combination. Best leave selection to the experts and know you were correct.

The book was taken back to the lounge where he sat and read through the chapter, assessing the relative merits as he went along.

At eight o'clock he would again phone Tony. The boy was bound to have finished at the gym and be home by then.

Tony's home had worried him too. True he wasn't at his most observant on the one evening he had been there, but it had been in disarray and the colours were a little strong. There had been one hideous picture above the fireplace. It made him shudder to think anyone would select such a thing. It was tasteless and the framing was quite cheaply done. Out of politeness he had said that it was "an interesting print".

Tony had said it was a gouache. It had sounded rather like gauche but of course he hadn't questioned it at the time. He had looked it up later and had had quite some trouble with the spelling. He had discovered it meant a wash drawing. He liked the word. He must remember it. It showed that even with an untidy flat Tony had something to offer. Gouache – it summed up the work's nasty accidental look so well.

They had a stiff drink and then coffee at tony's on the Friday night. The glasses were cheap, but the cognac very reasonable. The coffee had smelt rich. Peter had had to avoid drinking it because of possible problems staying awake all through the night. He never allowed himself coffee after five o'clock. He didn't suppose Tony had noticed, the state he was in.

It had been quite a surprise when they had been sexual afterwards. He himself had entered into it so freely. He had never done anything like it before – sex on the floor, if you don't mind, half naked in front of the gas heater. If his friends had seen him they wouldn't have believed it.

He had even put Tony's penis inside his mouth and sucked it. Usually the thought repelled him utterly but that night he had followed the boy's example and delicately run his lips the length of the erection. It had been a revelation. It hadn't tasted unpleasant at all, as he had suspected it would. He doubted he would want to do the like again, but was glad he had let his inhibitions go, just this once.

On arriving home he had gargled thoroughly so there was little likelihood of developing any nasty infection. It had been a week now. One of the girls had been sent out to buy him some "Massive C" and he had taken them religiously for five days to ward off evil signs. There had been an uncomfortable prickling feeling at times around his genitals. Surely it had just been apprehension, nerves. It had gone now. There had been no visible rash, just an itching. If it hadn't disappeared he would have been forced into seeking medical help; then in no time all his acquaintances would, no doubt, have found out. But

Tony didn't seem the kind of boy to have anything untoward. It was just nerves.

Nearly eight o'clock; he would phone again soon. He selected the desired menu and carefully placed the Florentine bookmark between the pages. Later he would copy out a shopping list from it; now he could phone Tony. It was pointless to go too far with the plans if the boy was going to let him down.

Tony just made it inside before the phone stopped ringing. He was breathless when he answered. He should have known it would be Peter. The last thing he felt like was indulging in small talk. Peter was a two valium job at the best of times.

Yes, he confirmed he would be coming the next night.

No, he didn't require a lift.

Yes, he was quite sure he could find his way.

Yes, he did have the address and the phone number.

No, he would be punctual.

Yes, he was looking forward to it.

He hung up furious that he hadn't had the courage to worm his way out of it. Peter was so organizing, Tony felt overawed when he was caught like that.

It was so ridiculous the way the whole thing had happened anyway. Two more unmatched people you would be hard to find. The only things they had had in common were loneliness and fear. Tony was coming to terms with the latter; the former still passed over him in waves. But then, as his doctor said, "No one is irreplaceable."

It should be true. In time it would be. His doctor was marvellous. He had summed up Mark in one phrase. "He's a prick, isn't he?" the doctor had said. It had allowed Tony to laugh and then argue in Mark's favour, enumerating all his own failings that had contributed to the breakup. In times of need he could easily love his doctor.

For a few moments Tony pondered the plausibility of going to him and confiding about last Friday night. The man had become a confessor figure so it would be quite easy. He decided against it at last on the grounds that there was nothing anyone could do about it now. The guy was dead. It was finished. Just like his relationship with Mark. Dead and finished. As he had bemoaned to the doctor, "You can't make him come back."

Not even a doctor could bring back the dead youth either. A revelation to the doctor would serve no useful purpose and only put at risk the relationship that he cherished.

Tony threw off his jacket and sprawled out on the sofa. He peeled off his boots and left them there on the floor. His dirty socks rested on the arm of the chair. He contemplated his socks and the weekend ahead. A desert, with Peter the only oasis. That was one oasis he must let perish back into the wilderness. He waited with apprehension to see the house. It had been described to him by inference all week. Peter was nothing if not proud of his success. The trouble was it was not the kind of success Tony sought or could relate to. He shouldn't have encouraged the thing to develop between them the way it had. Someone was going to get hurt now.

Initially it had fed some of the need created by Mark's departure; now he saw that even this satisfaction had been shallow. He was selfish to have let it go this far.

Sex had been the big mistake. The lift was necessary. He'd had to get away from the area fast. Coffee had been a politeness, the drink essential. Sex, his own desperate innovation to blot out the earlier event, had been his undoing.

He smiled to himself. During the performance Peter had graduated from shock to finally inhibited enthusiasm. It was because Tony had made the approaches that he now felt guilty. Having found this new attachment, Peter was sticking like glue and Tony had to admit responsibility for it.

Actually Peter had been rather sweet afterwards in a comical sort of way. The sticky aftermath of mutual masturbation had offended him greatly. Despite copious quantities of tissues and a shower, he had obviously not felt clean.He had paused so fastidiously before putting his soiled underwear back on. It had been a great compromise for him. There was something so vulnerable about his out-of-condition body revealed in the electric light as he stood clumsily viewing his own underclothes.

Tony held the picture in his mind for as long as possible. At least thinking about that was a diversion from thinking about Mark.

Mark sat outside in his car. He had waited for Tony to return from work. When he had finally seen him coming, he no longer was sure what to do. Within twenty-four hours of leaving Tony, he knew he loved the neurotic guy. It was just that he couldn't live with him. The tantrums, the traumas, the unpredictability, the lack of freedom: he couldn't live with Tony. He told himself he was waiting outside because he wanted to see that his friend was coping. Loving someone was strange. You could hate them and need them all at once.

He didn't know why he had come there tonight. Now he found it impossible to drive away. The jealousy and raging had gone on too long. Partly it was his own fault. He hadn't been completely honest, ever, with anyone. All the talk to others which had so undermined the relationship, had been part of his own need to be something special in their eyes. Other lovers had been part of his own ego-building, not anything intended against Tony. Tony couldn't cope with it. Himself, he couldn't cope with the showdowns. Yet he waited outside in the dark unable to leave.

Finally, after many minutes, he slid the car into drive and swung out onto the road. Turning the car at the end of the road felt like death.

Tony didn't have much idea what to do with the evening. The gym had been a fiasco. He could go for a run through the park. On consideration he was hesitant about going off in the dark. The park had been under close police surveillance for the past week. Several times they had trailed him as he ran along past the beats. On the Monday and Tuesday they had been pulling people up for questioning. Tony didn't fancy standing there in the glare of the flashing blue lights for all to see, while some cop decided how hard to harass him.

In prior weeks the park had become a hive of industry at night. Now the backlash was really on. Tony knew nothing and had seen nothing. No one had been in the park that night. No one could identify anyone. One person was much like another in the dark; everyone was anonymous. No one had seen anything.

Peter removed his glasses and held them to contemplate his choice. The avocado and prawns could be prepared well in advance. With lemon juice the fruit wouldn't discolour. The steak au poivre was awkward, but so suitable for only two people. The orange soufflé would demand his attention again at the end of the evening but would give such a good final flair. Such a pity the book didn't suggest accompanying wines. A champagne and a reasonable red would probably suffice. Tony didn't appear to be a heavy drinker, not with that body.

Methodically he copied the ingredients onto a pad, eliminating those he knew he already had. Once or twice he rose and went to the cupboards to check for one ingredient or another. It was worth doing it properly now, rather than trusting to memory in the morning.

Suddenly he stopped in his task. If Tony had no transport, presumably he intended to stay overnight. That would mean both facing a stranger first thing in the morning and planning a breakfast menu. Should he have the spare room prepared for appearances sake? After all, it would become Tony's room in time. He would make the offer after another week or two. Or maybe he should show Tony around for his friends' approval first. The thought nearly gave him cold feet. Tony there within a fortnight.

Placing down his glasses and leaving note-pad and pen, he went to his bedroom. He opened his wardrobe door and carefully removed a velvet robe. He must let it air properly before his house-guest was to use it.

In the bathroom he scanned the cupboard to ensure that there was a spare toothbrush. He knew he could match a face-washer to the guest towels. If all went well, and Tony moved in, he would have a set monogrammed for him. But what was he saying? It was early days to let such excitement get out of hand. There were more practical questions to consider first, like how to introduce Tony to his circle of friends without including details of their first meeting. Peter simply refused to consider the other aspects of their meeting. Obviously Tony was right for his needs and could be adapted into his lifestyle easily enough.

The boy was attached to his present flat for sentimental reasons. Once he realized that his previous love affair was over, he would see the advantages of moving out. It was, after all, a better address that Peter had to offer, as well as access to a far better circle of acquaintances. They would have to spend a little on the boy's wardrobe, buy him some reasonable clothes and let that funny haircut grow out, but the body was good.

It was time Peter had someone there to share his home and he had decided Tony was the one.

He went next to the second bedroom. It would be as well to put on the electric blanket and air the bed out properly just in case Tony would rather sleep alone on their first night. Since it was only a single bed, Tony could return there after they had completed the sexual part of the proceedings.

Peter then returned to his shopping list and carefully checked to see that all was included. He couldn't really say that he enjoyed cooking, or entertaining for that matter, but like most things approached sensibly, he could do it well.

He ran his finger along the top of the bureau as he returned to the lounge. The furniture hadn't been cleaned as thoroughly as he would have expected. He must remember to leave a note to that effect for his woman on her next visit. After glancing at the clock and asserting it was too early to retire for the evening, he again switched on the television and settled in to watch the ABC.

As the evening wore on Tony felt the confines of the flat playing on him more and more. He hadn't eaten and was itching to get out if only he could muster a reason. It was developing into a valium evening. He took two tablets without water and decided to contemplate masturbation. Sprawled out on the sofa, he ran his hand up and down his thigh and tried to raise some enthusiasm. It would be interesting to see which worked first, the pills or the stimulation.

He casually massaged his penis through his clothing and knew he wasn't interested. The squeezing and fingering had some effect in producing a swelling but his muscles were relaxing fast all over his body and his head was starting to follow suit. It was all starting to feel too much effort.

Unzipping his fly, he slid his hand down inside his underpants and released the early swellings trapped there. Massaging coaxingly he looked down and viewed the unwillingly roused object. It was a lot of effort and for what? True it was pleasant enough lying there playing with himself, but he had no desire for anything more. Like the rest of his body, it would be nice to let it just relax. He placed it back inside his pants and rezipped them. Remaining sprawled out, he gazed across the room enjoying the fact that thoughts refused to articulate themselves clearly in his brain. An idea would half form, then disintegrate. He wondered where the thought went, then that idea disappeared too.

After a while he rose and loped to the bedroom. Slowly he struggled out of the confines of his clothes and crawled into the unmade bed. He stared at the crumped pile of clothes, then switched out the light. He rested there happily letting his mind deteriorate until morning.

Mark stood looking awkward. He was on the verge of leaving.

"Good day there," the boy called out.

Mark looked around, then looked back. He didn't know the boy.

"What are you standing there staring for? Come over, I won't bite."

Mark took the few necessary steps hesitantly.

"That's better. Sit down."

Again Mark paused, unsure.

"Sit down, it's OK."

Mark sat and felt relieved. At least the initial stages were over.

"What are you doing here then?" the boy asked.

Shrugging his shoulders, Mark replied, "What are you doing?"

"Sex," the boy replied, "I come here for sex, mate, and you?"

Mark nodded.

"Thought so," the boy affirmed. He then continued, "I'm commercial."

There was a pause so he added, "I do it for pleasure too, but I'm commercial."

"Oh," Mark responded, then sat looking uncomfortable.

"Well, why do you do it then, mate?" the boy asked.

"Pleasure, I suppose."

By now Mark was unsure there could be any pleasure with this one.

"Got a cigarette?" the boy hustled.

Mark handed one over and lit one for himself. They sat there smoking silently. It wasn't progressing fast enough so the boy urged, "Yeah, I'm bi. I do it for pleasure sometimes but tonight I'm commercial. See I'm waiting for my cheque to come through, and I'm broke."

Mark started to rise. "I think I'll be going."

The boy put his hand on Mark's leg and held him there. "Never paid for it before, have you?"

Mark nodded agreement.

"Stands out a mile."

"How long have you been doing this?" Mark asked. He

was pretty well held in place and couldn't get out.

"About six months. But it's dropped right off. Commercial is right out now. Too many freebees around."

"Yes, you're probably right." And again Mark tried to leave.

"I'm hungry, man," the boy ployed.

"You'll do alright I'm sure," Mark retorted. By now he was on his feet.

"I'll walk you to your car."

And the boy was beside him as he strode off. Halfway across the road the boy stopped and suggestively dug his hand down the front of his pants.

"My dick's all caught up," he commented.

Mark made no reply.

"That your car?" he asked.

"Yes."

"Bit of a heap of shit, isn't it?"

"It's falling to bits like its owner," Mark responded.

Mark unlocked the door to get in. As he opened the door, the boy reached over and using the inside handle, wound the window down before Mark could close the door.

"Why did you do that?" Mark asked.

"To talk to you, man. Can't talk through glass."

Mark kept his affirmation to himself. The boy leant through the window.

"Well, you interested?" he persisted.

Mark shook his head. "I got to go." He started up the engine.

"Fuck you, you fucking cheapskate."

The boy thumped the roof of the car expecting Mark to drive off. He didn't. Instead he switched off the ignition. The boy's crotch was at window height.

Mark looked at it blankly, then the boy leant and looked in again.

"Yeah?" he asked eagerly.

"What's your name?" Mark asked.

The boy was vague for a second or two, then replied, "John."

"Like hell it is."

The boy's brashness started to return. "Trying to tell me I don't know what my own name is?" And he grinned.

"OK, John," Mark replied, "I'm sorry. I'm not interested and I'm sorry if I gave you the wrong idea, alright?"

"Yeah mate." The boy tried one last grin. "It's no loss to me. Suit yourself. See you round."

He walked off as cockily as he could. Mark wound up the window and drove off.

For quite some time Mark drove round and round the suphur-yellow street of Melbourne's limited night life. Finally he made up his mind and turned towards his old home and Tony.

Once there he again sat out in the street watching from across the road. Procrastination was pointless, he wanted to go back. He made himself get out of the car and launched himself across the road.

The flat was in darkness. He went up the dimly lit stairs and tapped gently on the door. Nothing stirred within. The flat breathed brooding in its deep sleep. It held Tony within.

Mark tapped lightly again. Again only the omnipotent silence answered. He stood there, the silence barring his way. Then he took a key from his pocket and tried it in the lock. It pierced the resistance of the door and the levers turned heavily in the barrel of the lock. The door opened before him and the darkness of the flat issued forth.

Mark called softly into the darkness and no answer came. He stepped inside and carefully closed the door behind him. It was no longer a violation, it was now an act of rescue.

He slid silently through the soft darkness of the flat to the bedroom. In the dim light from the half-open blind he could see the sleeping figure in the bed. Carefully he slipped off his shoes, then his clothes, and crept into bed beside him. Completely still, he lay next to Tony and knew he was home.

After what seemed like several hours, Tony's body

moved back towards him and, heavy with sleep, curled into the warmth it found there. Mark wrapped his arms around and cradled the man he loved. Only then did Tony awake.

He showed little surprise. His mind was still too fuzzy from the pills for him to realize the strangeness of the event. He understood the essentials: Mark was there with him, that was what counted.

As the night wore on and the drugs wore off, the spasmodic exchanges between them grew more detailed. At some time in the darkest hours around five, Tony sat on the edge of the bed and poured out his narrative about the Friday before. Into the chill of the night air, he sat with his back to Mark and spoke of the Bacchae of that night in the park.

He told of a young male torn to bits by a frenzy of avenging queens defending their lair as savagely as wild beasts. The crisp chill of pre-dawn heard of a murder free of any sense of guilt, of a killing that was both small and momentous in its meaning. To the cold sleet of early light, he told of a conspiracy of silence that was both ages old and new-born, whelped in the dark of night one week before.

Mark listened and understood nothing. He watched Tony as he sat in the dark; then when he had finished talking, he reached out and held the figure close in his arms. He had always in the past been frightened by Tony's flights of fancy, now he answered them in the only way he could – he offered his presence as silent support.

Even though Mark dropped him off, Tony was running late for the eleven o'clock aerobic session. Usually he spared himself on the weekend but since he had walked out of the class the night before, he had decided to make up for it today. Mark had declined to join him.

He grabbed up his bag as he jumped out of the car, slammed the door and was across the road in a flash.

"See you in an hour," Mark called.

Tony preened as he bounded up the stairs. "See you in

an hour."

They would all see Mark in an hour, picking him up. The sense of humiliation was replaced by triumph. The Tony who could hold onto his lovers.

He swung through the doors into the gym and straight past the desk to the changing-rooms. He flung his gear down without even seeking out a locker and re-emerged within minutes fully changed. The class was in position. Linda stood at the front poised to commence. She gave him a smile of acknowledgement as he took his place near the front. There was no time for his usual warm-up. They all stood poised, the tape started up and the class began. He didn't need his usual warm-up, today he was in top form. He would make it through the session without any preliminaries.

The initial stretching exercises went like a breeze. The music swelled around him and he followed time subconsciously. The line of his back felt proud and perfect, his balance was steady and the placement of his hands and feet gave each gesture a grace he was proud of. He held a low squat perfectly for the arm exercises and was then ready for the more invigorating run. How different it felt from the night before when he had been over-critical and defeatist.

The first run passed with him feeling warm and comfortable. His timing and precision had improved and his breathing was relaxed and natural. During the whole class his mind failed to wander. He worked his body until he became an outsider watching it reflected in the mirror before him. It stretched and bent, it jumped and kicked, it sunk into the splits or balanced inverted as was dictated.

The second run came and went without his interest diminishing. When the class finished it took him by surprise. He discovered that his clothes clung to him and he was coated in a layer of perspiration, yet his body felt fired up to start all over again. All around him the class left the floor and a new group eagerly shuffled into place. It was over.

He completed a few final stretches, more for ego than

necessity, then, holding his body erect, strode between the waiting figures and away from the floor. Linda caught his eye as he past and again she nodded and smiled to him. The changing-room was crowded. He threw off his clothes and went, towel in hand, to the showers. He was proud of his body today and was unconcerned about other eyes upon him as he waited his turn in the crowded shower block.

Once under the shower he suddenly remembered that he hadn't phoned Peter. Peter was still expecting him that evening and was completely unaware of the changes that had taken place. Tony would have to explain that Mark was back. He had no idea how Peter would take it. He should phone the guy at once. It would be better from the gym than within Mark's hearing. There was no reason why Mark should know about Peter. Tony felt no shame about the whole affair but there seemed little reason to complicate matters when Peter meant so little to him anyway.

The whole affair had only been something to turn to for reassurance in a time of desperation. Tony would like to have been able to say that Peter was just a nice guy, but that wasn't true. He suspected Peter wasn't even nice really, just very keen. And on what? He hardly knew Tony. Once they had seen each other, only the once. They had committed a desperate and rather unsatisfactory act of lust – no, not that, just sex.

For one week now Peter had phoned nightly building up his own expectations. Tony had not over-encouraged it. He had promised nothing beyond dinner once and that was only under duress. He wasn't sure they would even recognize each other on a second meeting, let alone have anything real to offer each other.

It had all been part of that night-sweat of an evening. The park, the waiting in the cold, the disinterest. Then that young queen rushing back into the bog being attacked. Something had snapped and the men had acted as one. Not one of them understood what had happened although all had taken part. Peter had later capitalized on that impulse to give Tony a lift home. They had tried to recreate that feeling of strength and unity through sex. It hadn't worked. It had taken something more than that to combine six strangers into a common act. Peter alone seemed to misunderstand the bond that had been forged that night. Now Tony would have to ring and tell him that any further meetings were off. Any continuation of what had been so unfortunately triggered off was now out of the question.

He considered a valium to make the call easier but decided it wasn't necessary. He could do it anyway.

Peter was preparing the oranges when the phone rang. He didn't like working in the kitchen and the interruption annoyed him. He had already severed the tops off the oranges and was in the process of scooping out the flesh. His hands were messy. The recipe book had recommended you prepare the fruit well in advance and rechill the mixture. Placing the ice cream scoop on the damp chopping-board, he wiped his hands on the paper towel and headed towards the hallway and the buzzing machine. Again it went through his mind that he must order a more up-to-date model.

His voice was crisp and articulate as he spoke into the receiver. Any hint of animosity or annoyance over the interruption was well concealed. Peter always prided himself that he was well under control. It was one thing that he was careful to observe always amongst his friends. No matter how much he felt the prick of their goading and bitchiness, he never let them know. It would be the same when he presented Tony to them. Tongues would wag but Peter belonged to a world that both thrived on pettiness and denied its existence. Every friend was a hidden enemy, every dinner party a well-concealed battlefield.

"Hello, Peter?" the voice called down the phone.

"Yes Tony, my boy."

He was pleased to be able to show he recognized the voice. They might at a future point have to do a little work to modify the accent.

There was noise in the background and Tony was almost shouting. Peter held the receiver well back. The words rushed out as Tony unloaded his message into Peter's unlistening ear. Tony had completed his apology before it started to dawn on Peter what the call was all about.

There was silence on both ends of the phone as the meaning penetrated. Tony waited. Then Peter spoke.

"You're telling me you are not coming tonight?"

"Yes," Tony confirmed.

"Mark is back with you?"

"Yes."

Peter paused and looked curiously at the phone saying nothing. Tony waited for the response. Nothing came.

"Peter," he called.

There was no reply. He began again.

"Peter, I'm sorry, honestly I am. It wouldn't be fair to come over now everything has happened. It wouldn't have worked."

Peter's face had drained of all colour. His body was shaking visibly with anger. For a few seconds more he could not speak. Finally, when he knew his voice was again perfectly under control, he spoke.

"Thank you for phoning to tell me," he paused. "You must be pleased your little friend is back with you."

"Yes, I am," Tony replied lamely.

"I can't understand why you are taking him back, Tony. Still, most of us get that which we deserve, and he sounds a bad lot."

Tony made no reply.

"Ethnic, isn't he?" Peter asked disparagingly.

"I had better go," Tony tried helplessly.

"Tony," Peter said.

"Yes?"

He awaited what was to come.

"Tony, good luck this time."

"Thank you."

"And Tony, don't phone me when it doesn't work."

And Peter hung up.

The anger boiled and seethed within him. That upstart of a boy didn't even have the sense to see what he had to offer. Peter's plans wrecked by an unappreciative youth with a bad address and no sense of dress or decorum. Sex on the carpet before a gas heater! The boy would never amount to much with these values.

Peter returned to the kitchen and scooped the mangled oranges into the wet-garbage disposal unit. He rinsed the pulp off the carving-board and placed it neatly in the dishwasher. He closed the recipe book and returned it to its place on the shelf. He wiped down the bench surface for odd traces of orange juice, then sat on a kitchen stool.

At very least Tony could have come over that evening to talk about it. He could have seen the house, shared a meal, accepted his hospitality and his bed, and known what he was renouncing. The boy hadn't given a chance to Peter and all he had been prepared to offer.

No one could do this to Peter. No one could do it and get away with it. He could be both influential and vindictive. He would reek his vengeance. And he had one ace card to play. He knew Tony's name, he knew the address and where the boy worked. Most important of all, he knew where the boy had been one week before and the police would be most interested. A phone call to the right people and Tony would have little to feel complacent about.

Peter rose from the stool and returned to the hallway. He browsed through his embossed directory and found the number he sought. Systematically he dialled with his index finger, then waited satisfied as he heard the digits register and the number ring.

Then suddenly he hung up. His face ashen, he replaced the receiver and gazed blankly at the passageway of royal blue carpeting.

He couldn't report anything. The loyalty must remain, for it was his own protection as well as theirs. The conspiracy could not be broken.

They were all in it together.

Friday Night, One Week Back

Prissie was frozen as he tried not to mince along in the borrowed denims. Really they did look better on Leigh but they were necessary if Prissie was to cruise without having his head knocked in. He was walking well over in the shadows of the trees that hugged the line of the back of the houses. Over to his right he caught a glimpse of a distant figure in the park. It too seemed to be making towards the toilet block.

Further ahead still, a car was cruising past the darkened block. It went slowly but with no sign of hesitation. As he watched, it neared the end of the street. Then a dark red Mercedes was purring quietly past. It appeared silently from nowhere and was suddenly there cruising him. The driver made an obvious inspection of the pedestrian and glided slowly on, pulling in behind the other cars at the bog. He was interested, Prissie thought to himself.

The interior light of the Mercedes glowed briefly as a dark figure got out and headed across the road. The second figure coming through the park was nearing his destination too. The two men would meet as if timed so by fate. Prissie walked on. Timing could be the all-important factor.

There was a slight hum behind and he became aware of a new car trailing him. He quickened his step, trying to repress both his mincing gait and his nerves. He felt very exposed, very obvious in his purpose, a solitary figure on foot in an otherwise deserted piece of road. Nothing else to do but keep walking and brazen it out. So long as it wasn't the pigs. Frantically Prissie tried to formulate justifications for being there at this time of night.

He felt the car lights dim and the car ease to a stop somewhere behind him. That didn't seem like a move the pigs would use. Fleetingly he glanced back. The glance was too quick to be sure; he just sensed he was being watched. The thought of escape spun through his head, then out again. He was here to take risks and take risks he would.

Again he looked back. It wasn't the police, the car was too old. He saw a lone figure watching from the darkened car. The head was a mere shadow through the windscreen.

"Well here goes," Prissie said aloud and started slowly across the road. It gave a less obvious opportunity to look back and assess the situation. A street light gleamed overhead. Prissie paused under it as momentarily as a bird in flight. It gave the observer a chance to observe. There was no point in keeping to the shadows now and facing a rejection when seen at closer quarters later. A face leered from the car at him. What calibre of face he couldn't tell.

As he continued through the last yards of parkland, the car slid forward using only dimmed lights to guide its path. It gave the act a ceremonial quality as the darkened form moved silently forward to its predecided position. Prissie had no need to look back now. Like an ancient sacrifice he continued towards his goal. Even on going through the gaping hole of the entrance, he felt no need to glance back. The behaviour ritual was set; both knew the procedure.

Inside the place was surprisingly crowded. An elderly man occupied one of the cubicles. Two younger guys leant against the wall, waiting. One wore a dark business suit devoid of style. A double flash of white shirt shone, exposed either side of his dark tie. He would be the Mercedes. The other seemed to be in a tracksuit. In the far corner a further two figures were engrossed in fairly advanced foreplay. They didn't pause to acknowledge his arrival in any way.

Prissie looked around into the gloom and felt awkward. The man in the suit was obviously interested only in the figure leaning near him, while the sexual enthusiasm of the more active couple left little opening for him. Prissie didn't fancy a mass impersonal grope. Perhaps what loitered outside held more promise? After all, whoever he was, he had selected Prissie.

He returned to the entrance. Outside in the bushes the figure waited for him. From what he could tell, it looked thickset and of medium height. Prissie took a step out of the doorway and the figure stepped out of the bushes. It was about ten yards off. The guy looked pretty straight. For a second Prissie paused. The guy took hold of his own cock through his pants, and massaged it gently as he jerked his head, indicating he wanted Prissie to join him.

For a second or two longer Prissie wasn't sure. Something felt wrong about the whole thing. Now the offer had been made, he could happily have gone home without going through with anything more. Sex, there in the open, would be both cold and sordid. Inside the bog was already too crowded. Yet he stepped forward towards the waiting figure. It was part of the rite that once started must continue through to its climax. Prissie stepped forward.

He was nearly there, when a muffled horn blurted out a warning from the waiting car. In alarm Prissie spun his head around. A second figure was crouched there, huddled behind the steering-wheel. Like lightning it dawned on him what was happening. Prissie was being set up.

A fist swung forward but Prissie had already started and was poised to run. The blow smacked into his jaw, grazing his cheek. But its impact had been greatly reduced by the warning.

Prissie heard himself cry out and blindly he stumbled back towards the dark protection of the bog.

The commotion of Prissie's second entrance sent the dark figures scattering to the far corners and recesses of the enclosure. Scrabbling desperately for the wall, Prissie clung to the shadows, repressing a stifled moan.

The next second Kevin was there howling in his pursuit of the injured queen.

"Come and get it, you bastard," he goaded.

The triumph in his voice proclaimed the victory he felt. Prissie's fate was, in his mind at least, sealed. There he stood facing blind into the darkness, confronting a lair, when he expected a lone, injured cub.

Tony moved in the darkness and Kevin swung around. Assuming it was Prissie, he crowed, "There you are, you cunt."

The blow he threw missed. Tony had moved on in the darkness. Prissie, the supposed target, clung in silence to the damp wall and stared back at Kevin.

Other figures started to move, looming in on the aggressor. His voice cracked in fear as he began to realize the pack that surrounded him. Lashing out wildly he cried, "Shit, how many of you bastards are there?"

Peter staggered back from the blow.

Gerry, Arthur, Robbo, Tony, Peter: suddenly they were all around him, touching and taunting as they began to unveil their hatred. Not a word passed between them as they touched and half stroked the frightened quarry. Then, as if by some hidden signal, all drew back and there was both stillness and silence.

As Gerry stepped back something cracked beneath his feet. Kevin swung around to see the shape filling the exit, his only means of escape. Kevin lurched towards the figure challenging, "You fucking poofter."

But the sound behind him stopped him where he was.

Robbo's lighter flashed and six faces were illuminated in the brief glow of light. In the stillness that followed they all waited.

Stepping forward Robbo raised his arm ceremoniously. It hovered high in the air, then he brought it cracking down across the boy's face. Kevin lurched backwards, stunned. Still no word was spoken.

Stooping to the ground, Gerry dug his fingers around the loose piece of cement that had crunched beneath his feet. Drawing in his breath, he rose again to an upright position. He closed his eyes and brought it crashing down onto the back of the boy's head. He in turn then stepped back. The figure reeled towards Arthur's frightened form.

His aged knee came up hard into the victim's groin as if the whole event had been choreographed.

Prissie watched amazed as figures moved forward in turn. A group of strangers preserving a bizarre sense of etiquette, as each in turn struck to destroy his attacker.

The boy cried out as Tony slugged his fist into the face. Arthur in near ecstasy repeated his choreographic knee to the groin. The body sank towards his knees, his arms raised in worship, in recognition of the event or to protect his head, it was unclear which.

Robbo's hard leather boot slammed into his spine. The body jerked involuntarily backwards. Its movements now seemed mechanical, not human. Peter's soft leather shoe echoed the movement into the boy's already injured groin.

Then all stood back. In silence they watched as the boy retreated, dragging himself inevitably towards the cowering Prissie and the dampness of the urinal. Prissie froze as the boy's hand met his leg in the darkness. Both remained perfectly still as if to deny their existence to the other. Through the darkness five sets of eyes burnt on Prissie.

Deliberately he lifted his hands and with the palms stretched back, seized the boy's head and crashed it to the floor.

There was again silence. The act was complete.